the white witch

The White Witch
'LIKE' us on Facebook
https://www.facebook.com/BCMorinAuthor

For sales information please contact:
bcmorin_tkc@yahoo.com

This book is a work of fiction. References to historical events, real people, or real
locales are used fictitiously. Other names, characters, places, and incidents are the
product of the author's imagination, and any resemblance to actual events or
persons or
locales, living or dead, is entirely coincidental.

Cover Art © by Aedo Morin 2015
Text set in Cochin LT.
Book design by Inkstain Interior Book Designing
Edited by Cresent Phelps-Borchardt

THE
WHITE
WITCH

BC MORIN

ACKNOWLEDGEMENTS

First thanks go to God and his son Jesus, for blessing me with the ability to write, creativity, and the gift of salvation. Thanks also to my hubby who inspires me, loves me, and keeps the kids from tapping on my shoulder every ten minutes when I'm writing, not to mention his complete enabling of my book obsession. (Yes, I am a lucky woman!)

Thank you, Tina Donnelly, Brooke Watts DelVecchio, and Sylvia Heintz, for always being a part of my process. You ladies are absolutely encouraging, brutally honest readers, editors, and friends and I couldn't do this without you!! Thank you also to Tina Týn, Erin Hoffman Dunbar, Marni Rost Jarman, Heather Lanier, Ashley Nicole Shelton, and Kelsey Darden for always being the first to volunteer to be my ARC readers.

Finally, a huge thank you to all my fans and supporters!! You are all amazing and keep me writing. I love hearing from you, and watching you fall in love with my characters as much as I do.

CHAPTER 1

Two more weeks. I sigh as I reach over and slam my hand on my alarm clock. Only two more weeks until graduation. I glance at the face down, unopened letters from the major universities I have applied to and shut my eyes tight. Thank God I get to the mail before my parents. Dad and Elizabeth would never have let me wait to open them. It's bad enough that I applied late and won't be attending any until the winter semester; I also feel bad lying to them and telling them that I haven't received any letters. I'm not sure I'm ready for the possible disappointment just yet.

"You up, kiddo?" my dad's deep voice follows the light knock.

"Yeah, Dad, I'm up."

"Okay, just making sure. Don't want you to be late, your keys are on the hallway table."

I strip the covers off and leap from the bed, running to my bedroom door and yanking it open. "You fixed it?!" I half yell, hoping my morning breath doesn't cause him to cringe.

My dad laughs briefly, and as I catch a glimpse at myself in the mirror behind him I see why. Morning hair, crooked jammies, and an overtly eager smile across my face almost makes me laugh, too. "Yeah, baby, my friend brought it over late last night. I went to tell you, but you had fallen asleep again while you were reading." His hazel eyes smile from between the black rims of his glasses. His dark brown hair is becoming more littered with grays and the hair touching his glasses tells me he's been pretty busy and hasn't made time for a haircut.

"Daddy, you're the best." I get on my tip toes, wrap my arms around him, and take in the Irish spring soap and clean linen smell that is his. I love that he is a broad shouldered man, no matter how quick the hug, I always feel like I'm enveloped into the safest spot I can think of.

He laughs, squeezing me into a bear hug and lifting my feet off the ground. "Yup, no more embarrassing drop offs at school for Katelyn by the old man."

"It wasn't embarrassing." I start as he puts me down. "Well, you know, not much, anyway."

"Hey!" He jabs at my stomach trying to tickle me.

I laugh and grab my keys off the table, my phoenix keychain dangling from the metal ring. "Freedom again. Muahahaha."

"Freedom?" My dad leans against the wall, crossing his arms against his chest. "Honey, you say that like you are some bad teen, who needs to get out and start trouble." He pushes off the wall and leans down, kissing my forehead. "Your idea of freedom is going to the bookstore, library, or coffee shop."

"Hey, don't judge." I raise my eyebrow, looking right into the eyes that so much resemble my own.

"I'm not judging," he says as he raises his hands in mock defeat and heads toward the stairs. "Hell, I wouldn't want it any other way."

I run back into my room, excited to finally have my car back. It might not be the fancy brand new cars that half the kids in my school drive, but it worked, well, again anyway and it's mine.

In my room, I grab my jeans, black v-neck, and boots and head to the bathroom to get what I hope will continue to be a great Monday started. I run my hands over my long brown, layered waves and turn to make sure that it doesn't look too much like I just woke up. I'd brush it, but let's be honest, if I did that, I'd look a bit like Diana Ross by the end of the day. Wavy hair was pretty, but with the right amount of humidity it could be pretty scary. After a bit of mascara, eye liner, and lip balm, I brush some powder on my barely sun-kissed skin and get rid of any shine.

"Morning, Liz," I chime as I walk into our kitchen and head straight to the coffee maker.

The smell of the freshly ground beans fill the room and I don't hesitate to take a deep breath.

"Morning, sweetie. You seem to be in a good mood today. Guess you talked to your father?"

I pull the keys from my pocket and dangle them in the air before sliding them back.

"I got your coffee started." Liz sits down at the breakfast table waiting for our morning ritual.

I pour the coffee into my favorite mug that is already filled almost halfway with creamer, before reaching for a toaster strudel in the freezer.

Waiting for my food to pop up, I sit at the table across from my stepmother. It still amazes me how my father managed to find himself a second wife who looks so much like the first.

Elizabeth Miller is five foot eight inches of extreme kindness. She is one of those women who is always so positive and full of energy, she makes you want to just hug the hell out of her, or hit her, depending on your own mood. Okay, maybe not hit her, but damned if she won't let you wallow in grief or a bad mood for a while. Her perfect big brown curls are pulled back into a ponytail today and she is in her jeans and a t-shirt from my dad's ice rink.

"Just two more weeks," I sigh.

"You act like school is torture." Her green eyes peer at me over her coffee cup.

"It is," I say dryly, before drinking down some of the hot hazelnut flavored goodness.

"Well, you can't hate it too bad considering you have all A's." She gets up as the toaster pops up my flaky morning treat.

"Just my way of ensuring they will never have a reason to hold me back."

More coffee.

Liz laughs as she puts my plate down in front of me, the fruit flavor filled pastry calling me to eat it in one bite. They always think I'm joking when I talk about school, so I just let them go with it. As long as my grades are good and I'm not going through some crazy goth or piercing phase, they don't ask too many questions.

"Oh! Ana called you last night." Liz gives a smirk. "You know, I really like her, she's sweet." Ana is our next door neighbor's kid. They moved in last year, much to my parents delight, since up until then I constantly gave them excuses as to why I wouldn't invite friends over, or get asked to go to a friend's house. With Ana being so close, they have successfully forced me to hang out with her twice by inviting her parents over for dinner. She really is nice and all, but I rather like keeping to myself. I try not to get too attached to anyone, not since fourth grade when my best friend decided to call me a freak in front of all our friends and never spoke to me again, well, not kindly anyway. Not my fondest memory.

"Yeah, she's cool." I shrug my shoulders.

I see Liz sigh to herself as she looks at me sadly. To be honest, I see her and dad doing that every once in a while, though they try not to make it obvious.

The rest of the morning consists of conversations of inviting Ana and her family over for another bar-b-cue, the universities I was waiting to hear back from, and my upcoming birthday.

I pull into the parking lot at school early enough to get a spot near the exit. Perfect, first one in, and then afterschool, first one out, just the way I like it.

The bleak and sterile halls have been practically wallpapered with flyers for all kinds of end of school events and parties. I look at my watch and see there is still half an hour 'til homeroom, so I walk to the back of the school where we have a collection of wooden and metal picnic tables for the kids to sit at during lunch. Seems like the perfect morning to sit back and get a bit of reading done.

"This is *our* table, nerd." The obnoxious voice of Samantha Cooke echoes through the empty area.

Goodbye, perfect morning.

"Last week, you said *that* was your table." I turn, straddling the bench and pointing at a table two rows down from me.

Samantha's friend reaches out from around her, knocking my book to the ground. "Oops."

I roll my eyes as I reach down to grab my book. "Very mature."

"It was an accident, Kay-tee. I'm sure Nikki didn't mean to do that, did you Nikki?" Samantha glances over her shoulder as Nikki and Samantha's other goon, Taylor break into a fit of giggles. "She was just trying to help you out of *our* table."

"Is there a problem here, girls?" Our guidance counselor, Mr. Wentworth walks over, only taking his eyes off me when Samantha begins her explanation.

"Oh, no problem at all, Mr. Wentworth." Samantha bobs her blonde cheerleader ponytail as she talks. "We were just talking to Katelyn about the book she's reading. I'm thinking of buying it."

"Really? *You,* want to buy a book?" The school counselor isn't fooled and I have to restrain a smile at the sarcasm. "Ms.

Miller, is that correct? Is that what is going on?"

Samantha sets her jaw and glares at me over Mr. Wentworth's shoulder.

"Yeah, um yeah, that's what we were talking about alright." I wave the book in front of him before packing it back into my messenger bag and a huge gust of wind comes out of nowhere, almost knocking it out of my hand. The sudden hard breeze prompts a confused look from Nikki and Taylor and gritted teeth from Samantha as she smooths down her ponytail, though Mr. Wentworth isn't fazed.

My heart beats hard against my chest as I pray silently that no other weather anomalies appear. *Please, not now*.

"Hm." Mr. Wentworth scrunches his brow at me and then shifts his eerily grey eyes from me to Samantha several times before deciding to walk away.

"You did good, Katelyn. Maybe I won't have to kick your ass for being at our table," Samantha sighs as she looks at her perfectly manicured hands.

"Whatever." I get up and begin to walk away when Taylor, grabs my arm and spins me around.

"What did you say, Fakelyn?"

"The name is Katelyn," I say lowly through gritted teeth.

Nikki walks up next to Taylor, her hands balled into fists.

"And... I didn't say anything. Nothing at all," I finish.

The first bell rings, letting us know that we only have ten

minutes to get to class, and I silently thank God for it. I use the welcome distraction to yank my arm free and walk quickly away from the outdoor eating area.

So much for having a good Monday.

I see Mr. Wentworth again on my way to homeroom and try to shrug off the shivers I get. He eyes me as I walk down the hallway and though I look forward, pretending not to see him, I feel his eyes burning into me. I've thought about telling my dad about him a few times, but never got the nerve to do it. I had seen him following me home a couple of times when I didn't have my car, but I continued to convince myself that the three years of martial arts I took when I was thirteen would kick in if he ever attacked me.

"Hey, I saw that you got your car back when I was leaving for school this morning," Ana whispers, as I slide into the seat beside her and take out my English book and notebook.

"Oh, yeah." I flash a quick grin. "Good thing too, I was getting tired of asking my dad or Liz if I could borrow their car or have them drop me off."

"So are you going to go to the end of school bash? I hear James Bancroft is hosting it this year and he has a house on the shores of Shippan." Ana glances at the teacher to ensure that she isn't being watched.

I tuck my hair behind my ear, "Oh, um, I'm not really into that scene. I'm not much of a partyer." I shrug my shoulders and open my book to the page Mrs. Landsley has given us.

"Oh, well, I'm not much of one either, I mean, I might go, I'm not sure." Ana drops her gaze to the floor as she shuffles her feet.

I think to myself and though I normally try to stay away from people, I think of the conversation I had with Liz this morning and go completely against my instinct. "I'm going to the Stamford Town Center this afternoon to stop by the bookstore before going to the rink. You want to come?" I have a flash of a ponytailed little girl with her hands on her hips yelling at me and calling me names, wind whipping around us, and water at our feet and silently hope this friendship doesn't end the same.

Ana's eyes light up and suddenly, I'm feeling a bit better about possibly having a friend. "Yeah! Have you read the new series by Patterson? Oh my gosh, it's-"

"Ms. Ortiz." Mrs. Landsley stands at the front of the class with her arms crossed, the sound of her tapping pointed shoe reaching us clearly. "Is there something you would like to share with the class? Perhaps you would prefer to be the one to explain how the seven soliloquies reveal the character of Hamlet and his quest for identity?" A corner of her lip creeps up, pushing an overly blushed cheek out beneath her straight black hair. Her eyebrow rises above her beady brown eyes challenging Ana.

Ana glances at me quickly and grins before beginning, "Actually, ma'am, I believe that they seem to reveal that he is virtuous, though quite indecisive. These characteristics are explored through his various ways of insulting himself for not acting on his beliefs, and his constant need to reassure himself that his deeds are in fact, correct."

Mrs. Landsley sets her jaw and she squints her eyes at Ana and me before turning back to the board amidst all the "OOhhhhhhs" and "Buuuurrrnnn" from the rest of the class, and hissing "That's enough!" over her shoulder at all of us.

I laugh out loud for a moment, relieving myself of the childhood memories and look at Ana mouthing, "good one." before passing a note to her telling her where my car is parked so she can meet me there after school.

The day goes on and I manage to avoid Samantha and pretty much most of the school population by disappearing during lunch and eating on the floor of hallway B while I catch up on my reading. I catch sight of Mr. Wentworth once more, but I manage to slip into a stairwell before he sees me. For a guidance counselor, he doesn't spend much time in his office counseling or even offering guidance. Not that there is much of a need for that here. Most of the kids in Shippan High already have therapists they see because their mommy and daddy don't pay enough attention to them, and apparently, the expensive cars they drive and expensive vacations they take just aren't enough. Just last week one of the girls in my class was having a fit because the BMW that she was given for her birthday didn't have a pink interior like she requested. *Really? Ugh. Two more weeks, Kate, two more.*

"Thanks for asking me to come along," Ana says in a cheerful voice as she straps on the seatbelt.

"Sure, anytime." I pull out of my spot and edge my way through the packed parking lot.

"You know, to be honest," Ana fiddles with her fingers in her lap, as we put more distance between us and the school, "I was starting to think you didn't want to be friends or something."

"Oh." I pinch my brow, thinking about how to respond to that as my stomach twists. "I'm not a very social person, please don't take it personally. You're cool and all, and I do want to be friends, it just takes me a while. You know?" *Hello, giant leap out of my comfort zone.*

Ana smiles, and I hope my response has satisfied her. "Yeah. It's cool."

"Lookout!" Ana screams as she grabs hold of the handle above her door and braces herself.

I hear the screeching of my tires as my heart drops into my stomach and my jeep stops just inches from the passenger door of a black Tahoe with windows so dark you can't see inside.

"What the hell? You have a stop sign, you ass!" I'm waving my arms like a mad woman and pointing to the stop sign behind them, but the SUV just picks up speed and keeps going. "Wow, couldn't even put down his or her window and apologize?"

"For real!" Ana puts her hand over her heart and takes a few deep breaths. "Geez, that scared the hell out of me."

Ana and I spend most of the afternoon in the bookstore coffee shop talking about the books we bought. Well, Ana did most of the talking, that girl never runs out of things to say. But hey, better her than me. Luckily, her mom's office is near the mall and she tells me that I can drop her off there before heading over to see my dad at the rink, which works out great because that way, I don't have to drive all the way back to our houses in the Cove.

I open the doors to the ice rink and take a deep breath. An unconscious smile makes its way across my face and I leave it there for a moment before walking in. I walk by the office and smile at Liz as she sits behind the glass organizing some papers. "He's got you up here today?"

"Yes, Connie is sick so I'm just hanging out here. Are you getting on the ice today?"

"How much time do I have?"

"About an hour." She smiles, knowing me far too well.

I glance in the direction of the ice rinks and feel the pull to make my way over there. "Yep, an hour's perfect. I have my final essay on Hamlet due on Wednesday and I want to get it out of the way tonight. So that works... skating now, Hamlet later."

"An essay due in the second to last week of school?" Liz clicks her tongue and shakes her head. "That's just ridiculous."

"Tell that to my AP English Lit teacher would ya?" I adjust the strap on my messenger bag and head to my dad's office on the far side of the building. I glance at the figure skaters practicing and realize that I will never cease to be amazed at the things they can do.

I have been watching figure skaters since I was six, and though I tried it out for a bit, I never really took to it. I'm sure the fact that I'm kind of clumsy didn't help my situation. But I do love to skate, so in between public skating sessions, and hockey games and practices, I always have the other ice rink all to myself.

"Hey kiddo!" My dad looks up, his eyes smiling. I look at his face and smile in return, the additional greys in his hair spark a memory of six-year-old me sitting with him, watching The Three Amigos and asking him when he 'painted' his hair white to be in that movie? He really did look just like a younger version of Steve Martin.

"Heard you hung out with Ana today," he begins, looking

back down at the papers he is reviewing.

"How did you-"

"Ana's mom texted Liz and she told me," he interrupts.

"Gosh, you'd think it was an event or something." I throw my hands up in the air.

My dad looks up this time cocking an eyebrow. "Isn't it? I just about called the media!"

"Very funny dad." I squint my eyes at him and scrunch my nose. "So, very funny." I slip my sneakers under his desk and walk over to the corner of the room where my hockey skates await me.

"All kidding aside, Katie," he says, looking up at me, "I'm glad you're coming around. Liz and I were starting to worry about you never wanting to go to a friend's house, or have one over."

"Geez, dad, you talk like I have no friends at all!" I wrap the too long lace around my ankle before tying it.

"Um, you don't, Katie." My dad's voice carries a hint of sadness.

"Just don't get too excited, I'm not about to call her over for sleepovers or anything, ok?"

"Fair enough." He goes back to reading the paper on his desk, and I make my way to the empty rink for some private skating time.

Almost two hours after having dinner I'm cursing my

teacher for assigning this Hamlet essay paper to us when pretty much most of the school is doing nothing but watching movies and having social time in class. "Alright, ten pages, one and a half spaces," I say out loud to myself as I press the *print now* button on the screen. "Done."

I lean back in my chair as the printer whirls away, inking out what I hope is my last assignment of the year. Of course, with Mrs. Landsley, you never really know. The letters on my dresser catch my attention and I get up, grab them and throw myself on the bed. I sigh and sift through them, looking for the two whose answers means the most. Harvard and University of Pennsylvania. I close my eyes and rip the first one open.

Dear Ms. Katelyn Miller,
We are pleased to accept your application to ...

I stop reading after the first few words and clutch the letter to my chest for a moment before opening the second and reading the same first few words. "Aaaaaahhh!" I sit up in the bed, trying to read the rest of the letter, but though my eyes are scanning the letters, my brain is just wandering to a million different places. "Yes, yes, yes!"

In an instant, my door flies open and my dad runs in with Liz close behind. "What is it? Are you ok? What happened?"

I begin to hand the letters to my dad, but I can't wait for him to read them. "Looks like I will have to choose between Boston and Philly."

"What?" My dad begins to read the letter and seems to do the same thing that I did, stop after the first few words. "Baby, I am so proud of you," he grabs me into a bear hug and the stupid grin I already had on my face gets bigger. "Your mother would be so proud of you." He whispers in my ear.

"Katie, that is so wonderful. I am so excited for you and proud of you." Liz beams a smile at me and waits for my dad to release me before pulling me into a hug of her own.

"Thanks guys." I let go of Liz and wipe my eyes before the tears get a chance to fall.

"Wait, does this mean you won't be doing the one semester at University of Connecticut?" My dad questions with a bit of sadness in his eyes.

"Nah, I already got accepted there a few months back because of all the extra credits I got in my junior year, so I will do one there while I get everything ready to go out of state."

My dad breathes a sigh of relief that I am not sure he realized he was holding.

"No worries, dad, you'll have me bugging you guys for quite a few more months."

"Good! That will give us time to make some trips down

there, find you an apartment, go shopping and visit the campus." Liz clasps her hands in front her, looking like an excited child. She really is the glaring opposite of the mean stepmothers you read about in fairy tales. From the moment she met me, she has been nothing but kind. Though I know I have freaked her out a few times and even hurt her with the famous "You're not my mom" phrase, which I immediately regretted, she never treated me as if I weren't her own. She was the one who told me that I wasn't a freak after my best friend yelled it in my face and taunted me with it as I ran out of her party. I always believed that Liz didn't see me that way because she saw what happened that day and still didn't freak out.

CHAPTER 2

It's a gloomy Friday as the rain hasn't stopped coming down since last night. There is a storm coming through and it has ruined most of Liz's celebration plans. She has spent the whole week talking about our trips to Boston and Philly and even started her own list of pros and cons for each university. Last night at dinner she was talking about the places they could stay when they visit me, depending on which school I go to. Dad just rolled his eyes. He is so used to Liz's overly advanced planning by now, that he just lets her go with it and agrees with whatever plans she makes. I was pretty glad to have avoided Samantha pretty much all week, but it doesn't look like it will be an option today. I park my car and sigh, knowing this is the start of a pretty crappy day.

"Going somewhere, Fakelyn?" Samantha and her evil minions block the door, as the rain pelts my head and I stand silently grateful for not having brought my laptop with me today. I'm pretty sure I'm not getting out of the rain anytime soon.

"Just trying to get inside Sam."

Samantha lunges forward and Nikki and Taylor take the post at the door. "*You* do *not* call me, Sam. Only my friends call me that, and you are *so* not a friend of mine."

I feel the anger welling up inside me. Years upon years of this torture that I had suppressed, tried to ignore, even tried to forget, come rushing to me.

"Who the hell *wants* to be a friend of yours anyway, *Sam*?" I spit out her name as if it disgusts me to say it. The rain drops come bigger and faster until virtually no part of me is dry.

"What did you say to me?" She steps forward until she is toe to toe with me. Taylor and Nikki rush beside me, grabbing my arms while Samantha throws her fist into my stomach.

The pain radiates through me as the sound of the girls' laughter penetrates my ears. Tears sting my eyes, but I do not allow them to come. I set my jaw, "Release me!" I demand through clenched teeth, and Taylor and Nikki let go.

"What are you doing? Hold her!" Samantha yells at Taylor and Nikki, but they stand motionless, their eyes devoid of emotion. "You see! You *are* a freak! I knew it. Just like you did at my birthday party when we were kids, you did it again!" She shakes Taylor until Taylor starts moving her head back and forth, scanning her surroundings in confusion.

"Those girls were bullying you and I was trying to help!" I poke her in the chest hard, causing her to take a step back. "I am not a freak! I didn't make them do that!" I glance quickly at Taylor and Nikki and my mind wanders for a moment thinking on whether or not that statement is true, but even if it is, then how? The rain falls so hard on us, I feel like it's going to bruise my skin.

"You're doing this, too!" Samantha spreads her arms out, indicating the rain. "Just like you did at my party." She pushes me, but I don't move. "You couldn't stand that I was getting all the attention and you got mad, and I don't know how," she shakes her head, seemingly still confused by what she is about to say, "but you made the water in my pool boil over, flooding the entire yard and ruining my party."

"What? Are you serious? How could I do that? You know what? You are nothing more than a delusional, mean, self-centered bitch who needs to make herself feel better by picking on other people and talking shit about them!"

I shove her hard with both my hands as a crowd begins to gather around us, some chanting Samantha's name, others chanting mine, and between the chants I hear whispers of some telling others to look at my eyes. "And I for one, am tired of it!" I throw my hands down with my palms facing the ground and a blue and white light flashes around me as Samantha, Taylor, and Nikki are knocked off their feet and fall to the ground unconscious.

Lightning and thunder fill the air and the students run screaming as a bolt shoots down and splits a nearby tree in half. I walk to the doorway where some of the students are standing and they all part quickly, fear and confusion etched on their faces.

I turn to look outside and see the bullies slowly getting up with the help of some of the faculty.

The whispers of the students around me are not as low as I would like, and I hear the words freak, weirdo, and nerd more than I care to.

"Come on, Miss Miller." I feel an arm wrap around my shoulders, but I feel numb, and devoid of energy.

"Mr. Wentworth?" I turn my head and meet the gaze that I have successfully avoided for so long. *Yes, still immensely creepy.* The strangest thing about him is the way he always looks at me, as if he knows something I don't, as if he is thinking something I should know and right now it's intensified tenfold. *What the hell is going on?*

I barely remember the walk to his office or sitting in the chair while his assistant wrapped me in a musty smelling faded blue towel.

"What happened out there, Miss Miller?" Mr. Wentworth leans his forearms on his desk and searches my face.

"Huh?" I stop staring at the ground. "Oh, I, I don't know. Samantha and her friends were trying to bully me as usual-"

"Wait. As usual? How long has this been going on?" He interrupts, his jaw flexing.

"Since freshman year." I lower my head and focus on my fingers that I can't seem to stop fidgeting with.

"Why didn't you say anything? I must have asked you a hundred times over!" He puts his elbows on his desk and runs his fingers through his black hair. He isn't an ugly man, but the glare he carries is unnerving.

I raise my head slowly and smirk. "And what could you have done?" I say with a huff.

"You'd be surprised." His expression changes and he is much more serious than he was a moment ago when there was a bit of concern in his voice. "Now tell me *exactly* what happened."

"Mr. Wentworth?" The kind old lady I know as Mr. Wentworth's assistant, opens the door a bit and pokes her thin face through the opening. "Sir, the police would like to speak to Miss Miller, and also, her parents are on their way."

"Thank you, Betty." Mr. Wentworth rubs his face and sighs as Betty closes the door.

I can vaguely hear her voice on the other side as she tells the officers Mr. Wentworth's response.

"It was lightning, okay?" The counselor's voice is firm and his eyes are dead locked on me.

"What?" I know I am a bit disoriented, but I am pretty sure that didn't make any sense.

"What you saw, what knocked the girls down, it had to have been lightning, right?" He furrows his brow at me.

"Um, yes?" I answer what I think he wants to hear though I am still replaying the entire scene in my head.

The door opens and two police officers walk in. The first one is tall with blonde hair, pulled back into a bun, her blue eyes stark against her dark tan. She seems a bit young to be an officer, so I assume she must be a rookie. The man who walks in behind her seems older by quite a few years. He sets his hat on the desk just as Mr. Wentworth passes by and gives me one more glance before leaving the room. The older officer pats down the salt and pepper hair that makes him look very distinguished, his dark brown eyes are focused on me as he takes the seat behind my school counselor's desk.

"Miss Miller, I am Officer Williams, and this is my partner in training Officer Grant. We would like to ask you a few questions about what happened."

I nod my head up and down, unable to respond as I pull the towel tight around my shoulders.

"We have talked to several students who were present, but we would like to get the story from your point of view. Can you explain to us what happened when you arrived at school today?"

"Well, I got here a little later than I usually do, so I had to park towards the back of the parking lot. The nearest entrance is through the Science Wing so I made my way over. When I got there, Samantha and her two friends were blocking the doorway."

"Why would she do that?"

"Because she's a bi-," I stop myself, realizing that I will have to tread very carefully, "a bully."

"Is that the first time she's bullied you?"

"No."

"Have you ever reported her bullying?"

"No point. Her parents are great friends with most of the executive staff here. No one would do anything anyway."

He gives a haughty chuckle, "I can't believe you would endure someone's bullying under an assumption that-"

"It's not an assumption. It's a fact. Two years ago, she just about beat the hell out of a girl who started dating her ex-boyfriend and she claimed that the girl fell down the stairs. No one questioned it, no one suspended her, and no one expelled her. Never mind that there were witnesses. After something like that, you learn to keep your mouth shut."

Officer Williams looks at his partner who is writing in her little notepad. "Alright, so say she was stopping you from entering the building. How did you all end up away from the building then?"

"She *was* stopping me from coming in. I told her that I just wanted to get inside, and I called her by her nickname, Sam. She didn't appreciate that and she stepped out to get in my face and tell me that only her friends call her that. I got mad and asked her who the hell wanted to be her friend anyway." Out of the corner of my eye, I see Officer Grant suppress a smirk and I finish the story, ending on the flash of light.

"What flash?" Officer Williams leans on the desk, his fingers intertwined.

"I don't know. A flash." I suddenly hear Mr. Wentworth's voice in my head. "I guess it was lightning. It knocked some of the kids down and then I remember another bolt hitting a tree and everyone freaked out and ran."

"That first flash, or 'lightning'." He uses air quotes when he says lightning and it makes my stomach turn. "Some of the other kids we interviewed said that the first flash of light wasn't lightning."

"Then what was it?" I look back and forth between the two officers.

"Why don't you tell us. The kids that were watching said that you did something to knock them down, that you assaulted them." His condescending tone begins to get under my skin.

"Did what?" I sit up straighter, not ready to be accused of something I didn't do. I think.

"That's what we are trying to find out. We searched the area where you were standing and found nothing on the ground indicating that you set anything off, but we also didn't find evidence of lightning hitting the ground."

"What are you saying?"

"I'm saying that a lot of the kids were scared by what happened; yet, no one knows exactly what it was that happened. Does that make any sense to you, Miss Miller?"

"No, I suppose it doesn't." I feel a heat rising in my body the way it did when I was getting angry with Samantha.

"Your eyes are hazel, correct? I mean they look hazel from here." The Officer leans back in the chair, folding his arms across his chest.

"Yes, they're hazel. Why?"

"Some of the students commented that as you were yelling at Miss Cooke, your eyes became blue, almost a glowing blue, much like the light they saw around you."

"That's ridiculous. Besides, I was barely able to see Samantha who was not more than two feet away from me because of that rain, how on earth could they see my eyes?"

"Fair enough; however, I'm just telling you what we have

been told, Miss Miller."

I drop the towel from around my shoulders, faking more confidence than I really have. "And how many of those students were able to talk to Samantha before you got here? Better yet, how many are friends with her? No offense officer, but she's got more people willing to sling mud at me in her defense than are willing to tell you the truth."

"And why is that, Miss Miller? Why does she hate you so badly?"

"I don't know!" Tears run down my cheeks despite my attempt to stop them. "She has hated me since we were in fourth grade and I tried to stop two girls from bullying her who she now says were never bullying her at all!"

A knock on the door breaks the intensity that had built in the room. The rookie barely gets the door open when my dad shoves his way in. "Katie!"

I rise from my seat and fling myself into his arms.

"Are you okay baby? Mr. Wentworth just told us about the lightning strike! It's a miracle that you weren't hit, being that close!"

My dad looks over at the two officers and releases me into Liz's arms. "What the hell is going on here?" He turns so that he is facing the two cops. "Are you two interrogating my daughter? My daughter, who is a minor and didn't have a guardian present?"

Officer Williams stands, clearly not ready to be intimidated by my dad. "Sir, we were merely asking your daughter some questions about what happened. Three out of the four girls in the altercation were hurt, and there are too many conflicting stories about what happened."

He looks back at me and then Liz before returning his attention to the police. "And what exactly is your conclusion, officer?"

The female officer puts away her notepad and glances at the door where the principal is now standing. "Mr. & Mrs. Miller, Katelyn, if you could please wait in my office while I speak to the officers."

"No." My father nods at Liz and she nudges me to walk away with her.

I don't want to, I want to stay and listen, and apparently so does she because she doesn't move us very far.

"That is my daughter over there, soaking wet, just having been interrogated by the police, and I want to know exactly what these officers have to say."

The male officer sets his jaw and I can see his frustration with my dad, and I'm guessing this whole situation. He could be out solving crimes and instead he's sent to a school to investigate an alleged assault by some teenage girls. Mr. Wentworth is sitting on a desk across from all of them setting his glare on the police.

Officer Williams begins addressing the principal, "Mr. McIntyre, to be honest, we do not have anything new, nor do we have anything to prove that Miss Miller did anything wrong."

Mr. Wentworth keeps his sight on the principal and doesn't flinch.

"In fact, Miss Miller is fortunate she wasn't hit or knocked down by the first lightning strike as the other ladies were." He finishes with less sarcasm and intimidation than when he was talking to me.

For a brief moment everyone is silenced.

Officer Grant looks at her partner with her brows furrowed. She moves her lips as if she is going to say something, but seemingly decides not to question the senior officer.

"I was under the impression you said that it didn't seem that lightning caused that first flash of light." Principal McIntyre rubs the stubble on his chin.

"Well, considering that there was nothing at the scene or in Miss Miller's belongings suggesting otherwise, we have no choice but to conclude that it had to be lightning." Officer Williams turns to his partner, "let's go, Grant."

As he walks away I see him shaking his head back and forth, Mr. Wentworth's gaze, still on him.

After over an hour in Principal McIntyre's office with my

parents, Samantha and her parents, the vice principal, and Mr. Wentworth, we walked out with nothing more than what he called an unsolved mystery. He said it was raining too hard and the students' emotions are running too high because of graduation to truly give an accurate account of what happened.

I was going to bring up Samantha's bullying, but considering that she was too scared to look at me the whole time we were there, I figured it was unnecessary. Though the principal continued on about our grades and what model students we normally are, I couldn't help but replay the entire scene in my head over and over again. I know that what I saw wasn't lightning and though I don't know what it was exactly, I have a funny feeling my guidance counselor does.

CHAPTER 3

The dream rolls in like a fog.

I am standing in the middle of the parking lot by myself with no cars around me. The rain is falling hard, but I'm not wet, as if it's missing me on purpose. Then suddenly Samantha and her goons appear. Circling me, taunting me. I hear the word freak, more times than I can count. Samantha tries to push me, but I don't move. It's like my feet are stuck to the ground. I feel the anger boiling up inside me again, like a tangible force trying to escape my body. Then come the beatings. Samantha punches me in the stomach, Nikki and Taylor punch me repeatedly in the ribs. I beg them to stop, but this time they don't and I still can't move.

They are soaking wet and yet, I am still dry. "Stop it!" I yell at them, and only Nikki and Taylor stop. Samantha steps back, shocked.

I yell the same words I had yelled at school and I throw my hands down, but this time I feel the surge of energy leave my body and escape me. I am surrounded with the blue and white light before it barrels toward them all, knocking them off their feet.

I bolt upright in my bed, my breathing uncontrollable and my cami drenched with sweat.

"Katie?" My dad rushes in and sits on my bed, putting his hand against my clammy cheek and forehead. "You ok? We heard you screaming."

Liz sits behind me, rubbing my back. "Were you having a nightmare, Lynnie?" She always calls me Lynnie when she thinks something is really wrong or I am hurt.

"Just dreaming about this morning," I mumble as I rub the sleep from my face.

My dad runs his fingers through his hair and lets out a sigh. "Katie, we didn't press you after we got out of school because you seemed really shaken up." My dad adjusts himself so he is facing me completely now. "Is there anything you might have been afraid to tell the principal or the school regarding this morning?" He looks at my clock. Three twenty-five a.m. "Or rather, yesterday morning?"

"The only thing I didn't say again, because it was evident in the story is that Samantha is a bully. She's been bullying me since after that party where she told me I wasn't her best friend anymore. It wasn't constant until we got to high school. "

Liz pulls me close to her, wrapping her arms around me. "Oh Lynnie, why didn't you tell us?"

"Because you guys work really hard to send me to that school and I didn't want to cause any problems there. So I just kept away from her as much as possible, and kept my grades up so that you wouldn't worry."

"Katelyn Elise Miller." My dad rubs his face in frustration. "How could you keep something like that from us?"

"Because I was handling it dad."

"By doing what?" He stands and begins to pace in front of my bed. "By isolating yourself? By not allowing yourself to have friends?"

"I was doing that well before I started Shippan High, dad, and you know it," I raise my voice slightly but am sure to not cross the line.

He glances at Liz and I hear her sigh.

"See, you do know, you both know. Something happened nine years ago and I can't explain it any more than I can explain what happened today." I stand and start pacing just as my dad sits back down. "I don't know what the hell went on. I can barely explain to you what I was feeling. All I know is that weird things have happened around me that I can't explain. And either you two do know what is going on, or you love me too much to let it bother you." I rub my own face and drag my hands back to my hair, taking a jagged breath. "All I know is that somewhere deep inside I have a feeling Samantha is right, I am a freak!" Tears roll down my face, but I wipe them quickly.

Dad and Liz come over and sandwich me in a hug and I just stand there and let them. Despite how I am feeling right now, despite that I have never been more confused, a peace tries to fill me as my little family cocoons me.

"You're not a freak," my dad whispers onto my head. "You are the smartest, most beautiful, most loving, and most sarcastic girl I know."

I nudge my dad with my elbow. No matter my mood he still manages to make me smile.

"We love you, Lynnie." Liz kisses my head and lets me go.

"I love you guys, too." I walk over to my bed and sit down. "I just, I'd rather not even think about it all right now, if that's ok."

"That's fine, kiddo, we understand." My dad throws me a kiss and grabs Liz by the hand, pulling her behind him as they leave.

I managed to fall back to sleep and not have any more nightmares. Later this morning though, I had to convince my dad that he didn't have to stay around today to baby me. He and Liz left early for the rink because they are preparing to host some figure skating competition and have to make sure all the vendors have confirmed that they will be there and that all the paperwork has been signed.

I take a deep breath, enjoying the silence of the house on a Saturday morning. The stairs creak a bit as I walk down and head to the kitchen. My favorite mug sits next to the coffee maker, with a note in front of it. I open the note and catch the two twenty dollar bills that fall out.

Thought you might want to swing by the bookstore today.

Love,
Dad and Liz

And just like that, my morning gets a little better. I pour myself a cup of coffee and make my way over to my dad's laptop that he left on the kitchen table. I punch in his password and see that as usual he had the news page up.

HEADLINE: Stamford rolls out the red carpet as business mogul L. James Blackwell II buys a 12.6 million dollar home on the Long Island Sound.

Twelve point six, million, geez, I can't even wrap my head around that number. *Oh well though, if you've got it, you've got it I guess*. I scroll down skimming over other headlines when I almost choke on my coffee.

Thunderstorms increase to record numbers Friday morning as several high school students are almost struck by lightning.

Great. Well, at least they aren't mentioning anyone by name, or anything else that happened for that matter. I shut down the laptop, suddenly disinterested in the news and head upstairs to change.

The weather is still kind of gloomy even though the rain has subsided. Quite frankly I've had enough to last me a while. After circling the parking lot of the Town Center a couple of times, I find a space that's not too far from the bookstore in case it does end up raining again. I walk past a truck waiting for a space when I am almost run down by a black SUV that apparently refused to wait behind the truck.

I duck between two cars and just barely avoid being hit. "What the…" I look at the plates and realize it's the same SUV that took the stop sign the other day. What are the odds that two black Tahoes would be cruising around Shippan, both having New York license plates?

I make my way to the SUV that just pulled into a parking space, not ready to let him get away with this crappy driving twice.

"What the hell was that?" I start yelling as I approach the open door. "You almost ran me over!"

"I am so sorry," I hear the voice call out before I even see the face. A pair of legs in blue jeans and sneakers swing out of the driver's side, followed by a fitted polo shirt over a muscular chest and shoulders. He looks to be about my age, though I don't recognize him from school at all. The bits of sun that have made their way through the clouds highlight his black hair as he sets his light blue eyes on me. His jaw is rougher than most of the guys I go to school with, making him look older than what I think he might be.

"You should be sorry. First, you almost make me crash into you a couple of days ago and then you almost run me over!" I huff, throwing my hands up.

He closes the door behind him. "Oh man, that was you? Damn, now I really feel like an ass. I'm so sorry about that too, I was trying to catch up to the moving truck."

I try staying really mad at him, but all I can manage after the apologies is frustration. "Look, I don't know how they drive in New York, but here, we try *not* to run people over and we pay a little more attention to our surroundings." As soon as I finish what I have to say I turn and walk away. I am pretty sure I hear him saying something, but I ignore him and continue forward. Ugh, probably one of these rich guys who think they can do whatever they want and just get away with it. I can't wait to graduate and get the hell away from guys like him.

I open the door to the bookstore and inhale. There's just something about being in a bookstore or a library and having the smell of the books with all the knowledge and stories they contain surrounding you. I walk over to the fiction section and begin running my finger along the spines of some of the books as I skim over the titles, taking some out to read the blurb on the back. After putting a few back that make it to my 'maybe' list, I start to look for conclusions to some of the series' that I am currently reading.

"Hey, so I didn't catch your name." The unfamiliar voice comes from directly behind me.

I drop the book I was pulling from the shelf and the mystery Tahoe guy gets to it before I do.

"Thanks, and you didn't catch my name because I didn't throw it," I whisper, trying not to disturb the people around me. I put the book back on the shelf and walk away from him. Again.

"Look, I get that you're mad at me," he follows me into the next aisle and a lady there gives us a sideways glance, "but I did apologize. Think we can start over? I'm new in town and the last thing I want to do is start off on the wrong foot with the first person I meet."

"No worries, I'm sure you can try to run over a few more people and meet them, too. They might even be more okay with it than I was."

He laughs out loud and I can't help but smirk at his laugh, it's sweet and pretty refreshing. "Are you sure you're not the one from New York? You seem like a pretty tough cookie."

My gosh, what is with this guy? I've been nothing but mean and sarcastic and he's still here. "Yeah, I'm sure. Just naturally sarcastic with people who try to kill me is all."

He laughs again. Seriously? Either this guy has one of the best senses of humor ever, or he is desperate for a friend.

"You aren't going to go that easily are you, Polo?" I fold my arms across my chest.

He looks down at his shirt and grins, "no, not really."

"So what, are you just one of these, 'I can't have anyone hate me type of people?'"

And, he's still grinning. "Nope, just one of these, 'wow, that chick is pretty spunky and funny' so I want to know her people."

"Spunky? Does anyone even use that word anymore?" I can't help the giggle that escapes me.

"I used it." He widens his eyes and opens his mouth, faking hurt, before ending in a smile. "So, what do you say, spunky?"

I sigh realizing that he is not going to give up. "Alright,

the name is Katelyn."

"That's pretty." He reaches his hand toward me. "Pleasure to meet you Katelyn, I'm Logan."

I reach out and shake his hand, unable to help the smirk on my face. "Pleasure to meet you too, Logan. So, do you normally stalk girls you almost kill in parking lots?"

He closes his eyes and takes a deep breath before setting them on me again. "You're not letting that go anytime soon, are you?"

I raise my eyebrow at him. "Probably not, Polo."

He raises both his hands. "Alright, alright, I guess I deserve that. So, Katelyn, what do the people of Stamford do for fun?"

"You'd have to ask other people in Stamford about that. I'm not what you'd call a 'partyer'." I end my sentence with air quotes.

"You're not? Hm, seventeen or eighteen years old, hanging out in the bookstore on a Saturday morning-" He looks at his watch.

Holy crap is that a Tag Heuer?

"Yep, still morning," he continues. "I thought you were the very definition of a partyer." He ends his sentence with air quotes as well.

I smirk and squint my eyes at him.

"Guess you aren't the only one who can spit out the

sarcasm." He smiles and his perfect white teeth almost gleam.

"Just watch where you spit it, Logan, I'm the only friend you've got so far." I grab two books off the shelf completing a trilogy I'd started and head to the register.

"Good morning, Miss Miller, just these two today? You know we are getting Kagawa's latest release next week and next month Chloe Neill has a release as well. Would you like to put a hold on one or both?"

"Not today, I'm good, Mitch, thank you, just these two." He looks at Logan who is a few feet away, perusing some bookmarks. "Brought a friend with you?"

I glance at Logan quickly and the corners of his lips rise. "Something like that." I shake my head and hand Mitch the money for my books.

"So where are we off to now Kate?" Logan leans in as he holds the door open, shining his bright smile at me.

"Well, one of we, thought it would be a great day to sit on the back porch and read a little before heading out to get some skating in."

"Roller or ice?"

I sigh knowing that what I'm about to say is going to make me sound like a bitch, or just plain crazy. "Look, Logan, you're nice and all, but trust me, you don't want to hang around me. I'm not a whole hell of a lot of fun, I'm not one of the money spending, party girls you might find in Shippan.

As a matter of fact, I don't even live around here. I just like their bookstore better. I live over in Cove. I'm just plain old Katelyn, with a plain old life."

He presses his lips together and nods, not saying a word.

We continue walking to our cars, though this time, the walk seems much longer. As soon as we start approaching, I click the button to unlock the Jeep.

His silence starts to eat at me. Logan reaches around me and opens the driver door for me, still not saying a word. I get in, put the books on the passenger seat, and put on my seatbelt. He leans against the door as I do all of this, all the while his eyes are scanning me and his brow is furrowed. "You always try to push everyone away, Kate?"

My heart drops into my stomach. I know that is what I do. Hell, my parents know I do that, but no one has ever called me out on it until recently. "Ye- Yeah, I guess I do."

He shakes his head. "That's a shame." Logan closes the door, gives me another look with a sad smirk and walks away.

The pain in the pit of my stomach gets worse and I grab hold of my steering wheel with both hands and slam my forehead against it. "Aaah!" I scream, though only to myself. *No, this is good, I try to convince myself. I still don't know what happened yesterday and I sure don't need any new people calling me a freak.*

I lay on my hammock, trying to read but no matter what

position I get in, I'm just not comfortable. It doesn't help that the birds are just chirping away in their cheerful bliss while my thoughts continue to go back to Logan and what I did. I feel awful for doing that, scratch that, awful is too nice. I feel like a horrid bitch. Then I start thinking about how I've done it to Ana, and I am pretty sure that I am about to see my lunch again. *I need to skate.* I need to clear my head and convince myself that not letting people close to me is a good thing. I walk back inside, leaving the stupid chirping birds in the preserve behind my house to continue their songs.

I get out of my car and find Liz outside with a clipboard in her hand, instructing some delivery guys on where they needed to go. This competition is a huge deal, I swear that pretty much every conversation I've heard them having lately is about the competition or preparations for it.

"Hi, Liz." I wave a floppy sleeve at her as I slide on my hoodie.

"Thanks again for the surprise. You and dad didn't have to do that." I give her a hug and a kiss on the cheek. I had texted them a 'thank you' earlier, but it isn't the same.

"You're welcome, dear. " She gives me a quick squeeze. "Are you doing better?"

"Yeah, why?" I shrug my shoulders and give a smile, but I'm pretty sure she's not buying it.

"You just look a little bothered is all." She smiles back.

Nope, she's not convinced, but at least she's not pushing the subject. "I'd better check on those delivery guys. I've got quite a few moms waiting on new blades and outfits for their kids. I'd tell you that your dad is in his office, but to be honest, I have no idea where he is right now. We have been all over making sure that everything is done."

"No worries, Liz. Do you guys need any help?" Maybe doing something good to help someone will take my mind off my own crappy behavior and apparent lack of social skills.

"Well, it would be really helpful if you grab a clipboard from the office, take a walk around the rinks and make sure that everything is up to par. Check on the bathrooms and make sure they've been cleaned, the Snack Shack area, ask Gloria if she got all the food she needed, you know, just stuff like that." She clutches her clipboard to her chest. "That would be so very helpful." She gives me a big cheesy smile that makes me laugh.

"You got it!"

I walk over to my dad's office, take a clipboard off the wall and start to make my rounds. Thanks to Liz being so anally organized and on top of things, there wasn't really much to report save for an order for more wine and beer for all the adults attending that had not arrived. I walk into the office again to make the call to the supplier and find my dad.

"Hey dad, looks like everything is good except that you

are missing an order for adult beverages that was supposed to get here this morning."

"Hey, kiddo, thanks. I'll give them a call tomorrow. There isn't anyone in their office now who could help me anyway." He takes a post-it, jots down a note, then sticks it onto his receiver. "Thanks for your once over. Now we should be all set. The out-of-town skaters should arrive in the middle of the week for the competition next weekend." He takes his reading glasses off and offers a weak smile.

"Dad, you look exhausted. Why don't you and Liz go have a nice dinner and go home? I can lock up tonight."

"You sure about that?" He begins putting away the papers on his desk, clearly in the hopes I'd say yes.

"Yes, dad, I'm sure," I chuckle. "Now go on, scat. Once tonight's skate session is over, I'll make sure that the Snack Shack team cleans up, John Zambonis the ice, and all the rentals are put back and sprayed." I put my hands on my hips. "See? I've totally got this. Out you go." I grab him by the hand and lead him out of the office.

"Hm, and I'm sure you will also be willing to test the freshly Zambonied ice with a little private skate session, right?" He raises his eyebrow at me and laughs.

"I will neither confirm, nor deny that statement," I laugh as I release him to Liz who was walking toward the office.

It doesn't take long before I get a text from dad and Liz while they are sitting at their favorite restaurant. I feel good about doing this for them, especially considering everything they had to deal with yesterday. I send a text back telling them not to wait up since I do plan to skate and maybe grab some coffee. My brain is still going a thousand miles an hour with my behavior toward Ana and Logan, and both of them calling me on it within a few days of each other. I mean, yeah, Ana was more discreet about it, making it about our friendship instead, but looking back, I know what she meant.

I need some ice time.

I walk around one more time to ensure that everyone is gone and that they did everything they were supposed to before leaving.

The countertops at the Snack Shack gleam and I see through the glass doors of the drink fridge that it's been stocked. I walk through the seating area and all the tables and booths have been wiped down. I walk across the way to the skate rental and find not one skate on the floor. Putting my hands on my hips, I take in the smell of the disinfectant spray we use on them and nod my head.

Good job, guys. I say silently to myself as I walk out and back to the office, though I will be sure to tell them that next time I see them. Though my dad trusts me to run the rink when he's gone, I'm sure he worries, so it's nice that the employees do so well and all without me having to say a word.

Alright, I get to the office and immediately start taking off my shoes. I lace up my skates, tying them once around my ankle before securing my bow and putting my jeans back over them. The light from my phone as I scroll my way to my music is the only light I have while I walk back toward the hockey rink, shoes in my bag over my shoulder. I remember liking the eeriness of the rink at night since I was a kid. I loved when my dad would shut off all the lights except for a few over the hockey rink, leaving it dimly lit. I turn for a moment looking at the darkness behind me. Hey, I may like it, but it's still eerie.

I insert my ear buds snugly before sliding the phone in my pocket. I stand at the entryway, my blades already on the ice, and take in the smell and the feel of the ice and cold air around me.

It doesn't take long for me to lose myself in the strides, a wordless epic soundtrack pulling me along. I revel in the cold air blowing through my long hair and biting at my cheeks as I cross one blade over the other, then glide down the ice before taking more long strides. I glance back as a strange sensation begins to overcome me, but quickly try to shake it off reminding myself that all the doors are locked. *Right?*

The sensation becomes an awareness of sorts and I find myself glancing around the rink, searching along the boards and the bleachers for someone. *Empty.* I skate a little faster and lose myself once again in the music and the feel of the ice beneath my blades. I begin a three turn and just as I pivot myself I see a whirlwind of snow following me, it is as tall as I am and lasts for only a few seconds after I turn. Almost as if it knew that I saw it, it blows away into the air around me. I stop in the middle of the rink and start looking around, my chest heaving, though I am completely unsure of what I am looking for. I start skating again, turning several times to see if it happens again, but there is nothing behind me. I want so bad to tell myself that I imagined it, but I know I didn't, and like Friday morning's blue and white light, it kind of freaks me out.

As I skate off the ice, I teeter between whether it would be better to just consider myself crazy or a freak! I resolve myself to going to see Mr. Wentworth on Monday morning. I have to find out what he knows and why he so adamantly told me that it *had* to be lightning.

Unwilling to walk through the dark back to my dad's office, I decide to take my skates with me and head outside.

I turn the key and shake the door a bit to ensure that it's locked before turning in the direction of my car.

"You know, it wasn't easy finding you," Logan calls out as he stands against the front of his SUV.

"Holy…" I put my hand on my chest as if it would calm my racing heart. "Geez, you scared the crap out of me."

"Sorry, that was not exactly my intention." His arms are stretched behind him as he leans on the grill, the muscles along his forearms are tense and his biceps firm.

Geez, this guy definitely works out.

"I see you don't confine your stalking to libraries. That's good, why limit yourself?"

Logan laughs as he pushes off his car and walks toward me. "Could be worse, I could be sneaking into your house, or watching you sleep or something."

I giggle at his reference to a popular book series.

The full moon illuminates the parking lot allowing me to catch a glimmer in his eyes. "Did you know that there are like four ice rinks in Stamford? I had to pick the ones that were closest to Cove since you said you live there and drive by each one to see if maybe I saw your car. And lo and behold-" he swings an arm to my car just as I stop in front of him.

"Logan, I have to be honest. Since we just met, I'm not sure if I should be really creeped out by the fact that you went through all that trouble, or really flattered." I move around him to walk to the back of the jeep so I can put my skates away.

"Well, I wanted to talk to you and I didn't get your number before you left, so all I had to get a hold of you was what you said regarding your plans for today."

I drop my skates into the trunk and slam it shut before

walking to the driver's side door where he is standing. He doesn't seem like a creeper. In fact, I'd venture to say he's pretty hot. Though I wouldn't tell him, don't want him getting a big head. A gust of wind blows through and his wavy hair is blown about, though since it's not too long, it doesn't mess it up. His chiseled jaw is darkened with stubble and he keeps moving it subtly like he is wanting to say something else, but doesn't.

I think again about what I said to him earlier and my latest attempts to step out of my comfort zone with Ana. Maybe it's time to try again, I feel my chest tighten. "So, Polo, what did you want to talk about?" I lean against the back door with my arms folded across my chest. *Not bad, Katelyn, good start.*

He smiles as he shoves his hands in his jean pockets pulling them down a bit. "How about we talk over coffee?"

I raise an eyebrow and hesitate, though most of me has already answered yes. "Sure. I know just the place." I reach over to my door handle and look over my shoulder. "Follow me?"

"Sounds good." He runs his fingers through his hair and smiles as he turns away, heading back to his car.

CHAPTER 4

I pull into the parking lot of a local mom and pop coffee shop I discovered about a year ago that sits on the waters of Westcott Cove. A faded wooden sign with a picture of an old coffee grinder with the words, The Grind etched across the top hangs from old chains painted in rust. The OPEN sign in the window is flickering and I can see that there are only a few couples inside.

"What do you think, Polo?" I question as I close the door and press the button to lock the car.

He walks around his car and makes his way to me. "It looks pretty cool." His eyes wander all over the front of the building and I see his brow furrow.

"Trust me?" I step in front of him, stopping him from going any further.

"Yeah," he smiles. "Not sure why," He squints, "but yeah."

I raise my eyebrow and smirk before turning on my heel. As we approach the entrance, I reach for the door handle but he quickens his step and gets to it before I do, holding it open. "Thanks." I feel a blush creep up and hope he doesn't see it. The only guy who ever holds doors open for me is my dad and on occasion a random stranger.

"Wow."

I smile at his reaction as he looks around, taking in the sofas, loveseats, and coffee tables on the right with small bookshelves in between, before turning his attention to the left where there are several small round tables with two to four chairs surrounding them. The walls are painted in warm browns and reds with murals of rolling hills and coffee fields. Out of the speakers I hear the voice of a sultry female jazz singer and I make a mental note to ask the girl behind the counter what CD they are playing. The outside of the building really didn't do the inside much justice, but I selfishly liked it that way, because that kept it from being some crowded hot spot.

"So, what do you think?" I cock my head to the side with a sly grin.

"It's very nice and cozy." He drops his gaze to me and his eyes meet mine. "It's perfect."

I feel the heat rise in me again and I turn away to avoid him seeing the blush. *Second time tonight? What is it about this guy? It's definitely not going to be as easy to stay away from him as with most other people.*

We walk over to the counter where a cheerful redhead beams a smile at us.

"Hi Katelyn!" Her gaze quickly shifts a few times to Logan and I realize she is trying to keep from downright staring at him. "Your usual?"

"Yep, large Chai Latte, strong with whip cream and cinnamon." I look at Logan who is still looking at the menu. "Logan?"

"Oh, sorry. Um, actually that Chai Latte sounds really good. I'll have one too."

I put my purse on the counter so I can get my wallet and Logan shoves it to the side.

"Dude!" I look at him as I try to get in front of the register, but he's already handed a ten to Michelle.

"I could have bought my own tea." I huff.

"As I am sure you have and will also do again some other time. Tonight, I pay. I was the one who asked you to have coffee with me wasn't I?"

I sigh, "Yes, you did."

"Man, I'm starting to think the guys in Stamford aren't very chivalrous if you aren't used to having a guy at least pay for your coffee."

I laugh out loud and cover my mouth quickly with my hand. "Well, some of them are, but I don't date much so I wouldn't know, outside what I see in school." I shrug my shoulders and quickly change the subject from dating. "We can go take a seat. Michelle will bring over the chai when it's done."

We make our way over to a loveseat in a far corner. It's a dark wine color with big cushions and antique gold buttons along the front of the arm rest. As we sit, there is an awkward silence hanging around us. Well, at least I thought it was awkward. By the look on his face, he might just be mulling over what he is going to say. He looks cute when he does that.

Dammit Kate, don't do that. You can't let him get close. Just friends. Just. Friends.

He sits and hikes one leg onto the sofa so that he is angled toward me with one knee on the sofa, his black boot hanging off the edge. He props his elbow onto the cushion sinking in a bit more than I think he anticipated. "So," he starts as he adjusts his elbow.

"So," I respond as I ease myself into the same position, with the exception of the elbow.

"You must come here a lot if you have a usual, huh?"

"Yeah, I prefer it to the trendier coffee shops. Besides, Michelle and the owners are really nice." I try to calm the butterflies in my stomach that begin to take residency.

As if on cue, Michelle walks up with two large matte black mugs each etched with a different design of a coffee cup on the side. I watch the steam rising from the cups as the butterflies continue to eat at me and take a few deep breaths as it suddenly gets thicker and rises higher.

Oh come on, not here, not now.

I shift my gaze to Logan who is looking at me and then back to the cups. Thank God, the steam is back to normal. *Phew!* I take another deep breath and try to calm myself. Though it doesn't work as much as I would like.

"Two Chai Lattes, strong, with whip cream and cinnamon." Her eyes continue to flicker to Logan, though I am not sure he's noticed. "Anything else I can get you guys?"

I look at Logan and he softly shakes his head.

"We're good hon, thank you." I can't help myself and laugh quietly as she walks away.

"What is it?" He sits up.

"You didn't see that?"

"See what?"

"Are you serious? She was practically begging you to pay attention to her." I reach for my tea and feel the heat of the mug as I wrap my fingers around the handle.

Logan shakes his head as he reaches for his mug also.

"Are you going to tell me that you're so used to it happening that you don't even see it anymore?"

He takes a cautious sip and puts the mug back down. "What do you mean by that?"

"Come on. Are you going to tell me that girls don't fall over themselves around you? And that on top of that, you don't see it?" I lean forward putting my mug down on the coffee table after almost burning my lips on the hot liquid inside.

"I don't know, I just don't pay attention to that."

"Let me get this straight, Polo. You're good looking. I'm taking a wild stab here, but judging by your car and manner of dress, you aren't hurting for cash, you're really nice, and you don't take advantage of or even notice the girls who fall over themselves for you?"

"So you're saying, you think I'm good looking and nice?" He smiles smugly as he grabs his tea and takes another sip.

"I'm saying, that if that's true, you are a different specimen indeed from any guy I have met around here, and I grew up around here!"

"Guess I'm just full of surprises, Spunky."

"Spunky? We're back to that nickname?"

"Well, I'm still Polo aren't I?"

I look down at the t-shirt he is wearing and it has polo

scrawled across the front. He follows my gaze and throws his head back in defeat.

"Yep, you're still Polo." I smirk confidently.

"Well, you still have spunk, so why can't you be Spunky?"

I wrinkle my nose and purse my lips, "I don't know, just feels kind of little kid-ish."

He looks me over and thinks for a minute. "Okay, no Spunky."

"Should I expect another?"

"Probably." He smiles over his mug and my stomach knots.

No, no, no. Not until I find out what the hell is up with me.

"So, you haven't told me what you wanted to talk about," I mention.

He averts his gaze and glances around the coffee shop before looking at me again. "Actually, it wasn't anything specific; I just wanted to spend time with you and hope you wouldn't do it again."

"Do what again?" I take a few sips of my tea, reveling in its warmth as it slides down my throat.

"Try and push me away." His face becomes more serious and the playful smirk is gone.

"Logan, I-"

"Don't do it. Don't do it now just because I mentioned it." He reaches over and slides his hand beneath mine, and pulls it off my lap and onto the center of the seat with his. "I get it," Logan leans in slightly as his thumb lightly caresses my hand. "You're a loner, you push people away because maybe a friend screwed you over or for some reason you think that to be likeable you have to be like the popular kids. And though you aren't like popular kids, it's not because you are weird or boring. It's because you're more. I don't know what it is about you, Kate, but from the moment I met you, I wanted to know you. I wanted to talk to you and hang out with you. Those kids, that idea of 'cool', it's a façade half the time anyway. I like that you're different."

You have no idea.

"I like that you're you, and whether you admit it or not, from what I have experienced, you are fun to be around and are likely a good friend." He shrugs his shoulders. "Look, I just don't want you to push me away. Give us a chance to be friends. I know this is crazy and probably a little creepy since we just met."

"A *little* crazy and creepy?" I repeat, pressing my lips together, hoping I'm not making him feel too bad after all the sweet things he just said about me.

His gaze drops to the floor where his feet are shifting and I see his jaw set.

"But, it's still kind of nice," I say, still trying not to make him feel bad.

He lifts his head, his blue eyes set on me and I find it impossible to look away.

"You seem like you'd be a good friend too, Logan." I can't help the smile that makes its way across my face despite the battle between my mind and my heart.

"So, is that a yes? You won't try to push me away?"

"Yes." I give his hand a squeeze before wrapping it once again around my mug. "I'm not going to try to push you away." I smile at him over my mug before taking a sip and a satisfied grin lights up his features.

Eddie Veder's ukulele skills pour over the speakers, as he tells someone he longs to belong to them. The irony isn't lost on me, especially since I'm well aware that I can never allow myself to belong to anyone with all this crazy stuff going on with me.

"So, what brings you to Stamford?"

He presses his mouth into a thin line and his eyes drop to the mug in his hand. "My mom. She was getting tired of New York and wanted a place where we can live but still not be too far from the City since my Dad has a lot of business there." He shrugs his shoulders.

"Well, don't sound too thrilled, you might bust something," I chuckle and roll my eyes, pulling a smile from him.

"I wasn't too thrilled, to be honest. At least not until

yesterday." The corners of his lips creep up.

Geez, like it's his mission to make me blush or something! "Do you prefer New York though?"

He shrugs his shoulders again. "Meh. It's not so much the city, it's more that my dad is always in business mode there and trying to drag me here and there so I know how all his businesses run and all that jazz. But considering he's been doing that since I turned thirteen, I pretty much know already. He just wants me to do everything his way."

"And… you want to do it your way."

He chuckles, "Well, everyone has their own way of doing things, right?"

"I suppose. Are you close to them, your parents?"

The smile is gone again. "I'd rather not talk about them anymore. I much preferred when we were talking about you."

"Wait, so you can stalk me, and ask me questions but I can't ask you any?"

"Trust me, you just don't want to know about all that." His voice, louder and more serious.

"Well, that sounds familiar." I try to lighten the mood, but the dark cloud that's appeared seems pretty heavy.

He laughs and hesitates for a moment, looking down at the half empty cup of tea in his lap.

"No worries, I won't ask any more… For now." I raise a corner of my lip.

"Fair enough," he answers, though he is still avoiding my gaze.

We sit in silence for a bit, enjoying our chai's and listening to Gabrielle Aplin's Panic Cord.

"I like her voice." I sit back on the sofa, crossing my arms over my stomach and looking at the ceiling. Though I'm not looking at him, I feel Logan's eyes on me.

He sits in the same position, but moves closer, closing the gap between us. "She's good. I like Eva Cassidy, too. Very soulful."

I turn my head, glaring at him. He definitely struck me as a pop or alternative kind of guy.

"What? My mom used to listen to her a lot." He turns his head too and our faces are inches apart.

I get a better look at his light blue eyes and am amazed to find that they are rimmed in a navy. I try to look elsewhere and I only drop my gaze down his nose to his lips. His lips are certainly full and for a moment I wonder what it would be like to kiss him. I instinctively begin to reach my hand over to him but stop myself. *No, No, Katelyn, don't do this to yourself. If you bring him in close and he finds out about the weird stuff that happens around you, he'll leave.*

Apparently on the same train of thought, but unwilling to abandon it as I have, he reaches over, tucking a tendril of hair behind my ear and letting his hand linger on my cheek for a few seconds. I wish it had been longer. He inches closer and I don't move. Let's get this straight, I know I should, but I don't.

"You are astonishingly beautiful." His lips are so close, I can feel the heat of his breath and smell the chai.

I have no idea if I'm blushing, though I might be, because by now my entire body temperature has risen by at least ten degrees.

"Logan," I whisper because it's the only thing I can do, for the life of me, I cannot move.

He smiles, pulling back just a bit as he touches my face again. "I know, too much for friends. I'm sorry."

A wavy tendril escapes and falls on his forehead and this time I reach forward and move it.

"I should get going," I say, my voice practically a whisper as push myself off to stand.

"Oh, already?" He leans away from me and I begin to feel a knot in my stomach.

"Well, maybe I can stay a bit longer." I look at my watch and bite my lip as I mull over this weird situation and the equally weird wave of feelings. I sit back down and give him a smirk. "So will you tell me about school or is that off limits too?"

"Very funny." He raises an eyebrow at me before continuing. "I just finished my bachelor's in business at

Cornell."

"Woah, wait, how old are you?"

"Twenty. I finished high school early and jumped right into the university, since I had already gathered some college credit. Told you, my dad doesn't kid around when it comes to business." He furrows his brow and purses his lips a bit. "How old are you?"

"Seventeen, but my birthday is coming up." I sit up a bit taller.

"When's your birthday?"

"Next Friday, graduation day."

"Ah, the big one-eight, have anything planned?"

"Not really, dad and Liz have a big ice skating competition at the rink that weekend, so Liz wanted to celebrate tomorrow along with celebrating my acceptance into Harvard and University of Pennsylvania. Although, knowing Liz there will be a birthday breakfast or dinner next weekend, too."

He smiles and nods his head. "That's impressive, do you know which one you'd rather attend?"

"Not sure yet. I'll do a semester here before I decide." I look down at my hands as I fidget with my fingers.

"So, Liz? I'm guessing she's your stepmom?"

I chuckle, "Yeah, she's really cool. Never really pressed the whole 'you can call me mom' thing on me."

"That is cool. What about your real mom, do you guys get along that well, too?"

I drop my gaze back to my fingers "She's-" I hesitate for a moment, "she passed away giving birth to me."

Logan hangs his head. "Dammit Kate, I'm sorry, I-"

"No worries, you couldn't have known." I interrupt before he can get angry with himself for asking. "My dad says I look just like her and that my personality is a lot like hers so we probably would have gotten along," I pause again, not even knowing why I'm divulging this to him. "Well, it *was* like hers. She was very outgoing and sweet."

"Hey," Logan puts his thumb and forefinger on my chin turning my face towards him. "You are very outgoing and sweet, too. I think you just take a while to let people in, that's all."

I offer a weak smile as an empty sadness overcomes me. "I just wish I could have had the chance to know her, you know?" I glance outside and a sudden wind has picked up, rattling the branches in the trees and yanking the leaves from their home, sending them on their way. In the distance, I see two eyes looking at me. They belong to a tall man, wearing a trench coat. From here, I can see that his hair is dark, and the stare is terrifying. *No, it can't be.* I close my eyes and when I look again, Mr. Wentworth is gone.

Logan puts his arm around me, pulling me in for a quick

hug, and bringing me back to the moment at hand. "I'm sorry."

I take another glance at the now empty tree lot. *Must be my crazy emotions.*

I wipe the tears from my eyes before they have a chance to fall. "I've never talked to anyone about her. Well, except my dad, and Liz once." I sit up and face him. "Sorry, I didn't mean to rain on our conversation."

"You didn't rain on the conversation. In fact, I'm honored you felt that you could talk to me." He reaches over and slides my hair off my shoulder and onto my back, freeing my cheek for him to touch.

It ends too soon as the phone in his pocket buzzes and he reaches for it.

I barely get a glimpse of the ID before he slides it open, approving the call. "Yeah, mom." He runs his fingers through his hair and sighs. "No. I told you I don't want to be there." He listens for a moment, but his intense gaze is on the ground. "I don't understand why he has to be leading the meeting anyway." He steals a glance at me. "I don't care if dad gets mad," he says through gritted teeth. "Yes. Bye," he sighs again before turning his attention back to me. "Sorry about that. My dad wanted me at-" he hesitates, "this meeting, but I don't want to be there."

"Oh. It's ok, no need to apologize. I'm not keeping you

from going, am I?"

"No! No, It's tomorrow, but regardless, I'm not attending."

"Oh."

Michelle comes over asking about another order and Logan convinces me to stay longer. I can only imagine the look of shock that will come over dad and Liz's faces as they read my text about having coffee with a friend. They immediately text me back telling me to have fun and that it's ok to be late. *Shocker.*

We manage to keep the conversations to books and hockey, though I'd be lying if I said that his demeanor during the phone conversation didn't worry me. He looked really bothered by whatever was going to be happening at that meeting.

At about one in the morning I decide that I should head home. For real this time.

"Alright, I suppose I'll have to give in this time." Logan gives me a weak smile, but it won't work.

"Yes, you will have to give in."

We walk outside and I am surprised that there is not even a breeze considering the crazy wind that was beating about earlier.

"Thank you for the tea," I begin as Logan reaches for the handle of my jeep door.

"It was my pleasure." He inches closer and I'm not sure I

can stop myself a second time from kissing him.

What the heck is going on with me? I just met this guy!

He leans his head down so he's looking right in my eyes and just barely slides past my lips, giving me a kiss on the cheek. My entire body sighs collectively and I remind myself that it's a good thing. Keeping his lips close to my ear he whispers, "When can I see you again, Angel?"

"Angel?" my voice comes out breathier than I anticipate.

Logan pulls back just enough to look in my eyes. "Yeah, Angel. You're the saving grace of this place for me." He gives a wicked grin. "Better than Spunky?"

I laugh out loud and can't keep the smile from my face. "Yes, much better than Spunky."

"You still haven't answered my question."

"I'm not really sure." I take a step back. "Not sure how tomorrow is going to go. I'll give you a call though." *Plus, I don't know how to feel about the fact that I am so comfortable around you. I've done too good of a job keeping everyone away for it to change overnight.* I add in my head.

Logan hands me his phone after he lists me as Angel (Katelyn Miller) in his contacts. I give him a grin and punch in my number. It's not long after I get in my car and pull out of the parking lot, that I get a text.

Hey Angel, had a great time. Thank U.

I can't help the goofy smile that spreads its way across my face, again. Yeah, this isn't going to be easy.

CHAPTER 5

I start the day with a good morning text from Logan that leaves me smiling. The afternoon is spent at the rink with Dad and Liz with only a couple of skating sessions for me, squeezed in between trainings and hockey.

My birthday and university acceptance celebration takes longer than I had wanted, but by nine o'clock Ana and her parents have gone home and Dad and Liz have resigned themselves to their room for the night. I had yet another nightmare last night about the light, only this time I was in a forest I didn't recognize and I was completely alone. It's plagued me all day and I decide to do some research.

I type in white and blue lights and get nothing but

decorative string lights. *Nope, not what I am looking for.* I stare at the search screen for at least ten minutes trying to figure out what I could even call that, but come up with nothing. So I go a different route and search Mr. Gamaliel Wentworth. Nothing. Not a high school picture, not a college picture or degree of studies, nothing.

Great, my discovery of more questions instead of answers leaves me staring at my ceiling for over an hour before finally fading into sleep.

I wake up after a night of completely broken sleep, pull my hair into a long ponytail of brown waves, ignore the dark circles under my eyes, rush through breakfast, and make a mad dash to school. I am hoping to get there with enough time to avoid Samantha and confront Mr. Wentworth.

As soon as I walk through the doors, the glares and whispering begin. *Great! Just what I needed.* I ignore them as I have managed to do for so long and head to the main office.

Mr. Wentworth's assistant has already left for vacation, so I head directly to the peach colored door with the standard gold plate marking it as the Guidance Counselor's office.

"Come in, Ms. Miller," the voice from the other side is confident.

I stand dumbfounded dropping my hand down to the handle and twisting it.

"I didn't even get to knock," I begin as I open the door.

"How did you-"

"Wild guess." he interjected with a sly grin. "Please close the door behind you." He sighs, "I'm assuming you aren't here for anything school related."

I squint my eyes at him, unsure if I should trust him at all, but realizing I have no alternative. "You're right." I pull my messenger bag up and rest it on my lap as I take a seat. "What happened the other day?"

He leans forward and puts his elbows on his desk. "You tell me, you were there."

"I'm well aware of my presence there, sir, but regardless, I have a distinct feeling that you know something I don't." I look for some sort of reaction, but when he doesn't say anything, I continue. "When I was in your office and the police were right outside your door, you told me that the first light I saw had to be lightning, like you didn't want me to give the police any other option. Why?"

"Because if they thought it was anything else, you could likely be in trouble."

"Like what though? I mean, you think it is something else, don't you?" My leg starts bobbing up and down and I feel the anxiety welling up inside me.

He looks at me with his brows slightly furrowed and opens his mouth for a moment before closing it again. I almost feel like he is waiting for me to say something that will trigger what he wants to say to me. "What do you think it was, or could be, Ms. Miller? Can I call you Katelyn?"

"Yes, Katelyn is fine. I just don't know. I didn't set anything off and I don't think anyone else did either, and to be honest, I don't think it was lightning at all." I prop my elbows on my lap and bury my face in my hands as the first bell rings.

"Don't worry about the class, I'll give you a pass for being late."

"I need you to figure this out, Katelyn. I need you to really consider what happened, what you may have done, intentional or not."

"Wait, what do you mean intentional or not? You think I did something!"

"Oh, I know you did. It had to come from you." He takes out his notepad and begins to scribble out my late pass. "Sometimes you have to think beyond reason. Is this the first time something unexplainable has happened to you?"

I stare at him, unable to respond. Mr. Wentworth just shakes his head as if he knew the answer to that before he even asked me. "I have to go," I say numbly. I take my late note off his desk and leave the office.

Taking into consideration the fog I am in, it becomes quite easy to ignore the whispers. Though there are a few who have congratulated me and tried shaking my hand. As I approach homeroom, I see Samantha heading towards me. I brace myself for the inevitable 'fakelyn' comments and endless torment, but she quickly tears her eyes away from me and turns down a hallway. *Is she afraid of me?*

After classes filled with movies and 'social time', I decide to head to the beach to clear my head. *Think beyond reason. Pfft. What the hell is that supposed to mean?* He's being so cryptic. I realize that I forgot to ask why there is no trace of him online and make a mental note to ask him the next time I see him.

I stop for gas by the Westpoint Beach Club and see a black Tahoe parked across the way at a sandwich shop. Though I know it's a long shot, I head over to see if it's Logan. Sure enough, as I pull up I see him standing by the truck, arguing with an older gentleman. He is a bit taller than Logan, which would probably put him at six-three or six-four, he has brownish-red hair pulled back into a ponytail. From what I can see from the parking spot I pull into, he seems to be very serious, a permanent furrow in his brow mars his thin face.

I step out of the car, but wonder if I should walk over since they seem very intense in conversation. However, as soon as I am about to step back, Logan looks over. Not around the lot, not in my general direction, but right at me, as if he knew that I was right there.

He smiles at me, but it's halfhearted and he nudges his head for me to come over.

"I will tell you for the last time, Erebos. I have no intention of attending the meeting. Good day."

I walk up and feel that I am invading a deeply personal conversation. The older man, I now know as Erebos, looks me over slowly, squinting a bit when he looks at my face.

"Hi, I didn't mean to interrupt, I just saw your car, and thought-" I drop off as he shakes his head.

"You aren't interrupting. Erebos was just leaving."

The older man sets his jaw, inclines his head to us, and turns on his heel to leave, though not without a huff.

"Business?" I ask, turning my attention to Logan.

"Yeah, something like that." He smiles at me and his eyes soften.

"Is his name really Erebos? As in, the personification of primordial darkness in the Greek legends?"

"Yep, primordial darkness definitely describes him."

"Sounds like he's loads of fun." I press my lips and shoot a glance over my shoulder to see Erebos pull out of a parking spot in a black Mercedes.

"Oh, yeah," Logan rolls his eyes. "Regular party animal," He finishes with a laugh as he leans closer, giving me a kiss on the cheek. "Sorry Angel, didn't properly say hello when you walked up."

I smile and don't have to look away since the sun is shining down and my cheeks are already red. "You clean up very nice there, Polo." I step back and look him over. The black dress slacks he has on fit him nicely as does the black button down dress shirt. He looks like he just stepped off the cover of a GQ magazine. His hair is gelled back, but still looks soft and touchable.

"Why, thank you." He strikes a pose, then laughs it off. "Are you hungry? They have great sandwiches here." He jams a thumb at the restaurant behind him.

"Oh, no, I was just heading to the beach for a bit."

Logan looks me over. "You're going to change there?" He asks, his gaze falling back to my jeans.

"Oh, no, not swimming, I just wanted to go and clear my head. I can't go skating because there are some classes going on right now." I point at the gas station I just left. "I was actually, just putting gas in my car when I saw the Tahoe and thought I'd see if it was yours so I can say hi."

"I see this stalking thing is catchy." His lips pull into a wry grin. "Looks like your beach afternoon won't be lasting too long, though."

I look out to the horizon and despite the fact that the whole day had been clear, I see dark clouds rolling in pretty quickly. "Well, so much for that. Guess I'll go home."

"You sure? We can go somewhere together, if you'd like." He gives a sexy crooked smile.

"I'm sure. I just needed to be alone for a bit, but I guess

I'll do it at home."

Logan slides his hand into mine. "You ok?"

"Yeah, just have a lot going on, is all." I smile, but I can see he isn't buying it.

"If you say so. Will you at least text me later and let me know how you're doing?" He steps close, leaning his head down and pressing his forehead to mine.

"Yes," I breathe. I feel a pull to throw myself into his arms but resist, hard.

The breeze in my back yard rolls over me, giving a small reprieve from the hot sun, which, despite the clouds that are rolling in, is still shining. I sway with one leg draping off the hammock mulling over Mr. Wentworth's words. *Beyond reason.*

"Hey, Kate!" Ana's voice drifts over the fence as her Scottish terrier sits next to her staring at me.

"Hey, Ana!" I get up and walk over to the fence. Her dog cocks his head at me, but otherwise, does not move.

"That's weird. Oliver is usually all over the yard as soon as we come outside."

"Maybe he just likes me," I say, though I am also wondering what the dog sees or thinks. I've heard that they can sense things… unexplainable things.

"You alright? You seemed really distracted in school today." She bites her lip before continuing. "I was going to text you, but I wasn't sure if maybe you just needed time alone."

I'm taken aback by her noticing my demeanor. "Thanks, just had a lot on my mind lately."

"Psh, I know what you mean. School, college, parents. It all just kind of culminates at this time, huh?"

I feel the sun burning my skin and I look up to find the clouds dissipating. "Weird."

"Huh?" Ana follows my gaze to the sky. "Oh yeah, that's so strange right? It was a perfect day and out of nowhere all these clouds just bombarded the sky."

"Yeah, strange." I bring my gaze back to Ana. "Hey, thanks for worrying about me today. That's cool and I appreciate it." OK, maybe it's not too bad out here along the edge of my comfort zone.

Ana smiles. "Anytime. I know you aren't big on having people around you, but if you ever want to talk or just hangout, I'm here."

"Thanks. Maybe some coffee later tonight?"

Ana nods her head. "Sounds great." She glanced down to find that Oliver has finally left her side to roam the backyard. "Well, I have to go run some errands, but I'll text you later for the coffee."

"Sounds good." I smile as I walk away and for the first time in a long time the thought of having a friend appeals to me. Not that it didn't with Logan, but that wasn't just a feeling of friendship. Despite me fighting it, there is a strangely powerful draw to be near him.

Lying again on the hammock I fall back to my previous thoughts. I start to think back to every time something immensely strange has happened and try to find common denominators. So far, the only connection I can make is that I was very emotional. Last Friday, Samantha's birthday party, and little things like the whirlwind of snowflakes and ice at the rink on Saturday night. Even all the smaller things that others may not notice, like the crazy gust of wind, the steam from the chai or even the sudden clouds today happened when something pretty emotional was happening. Most people would just think of all that as a weird coincidence, but I know better.

My attention is suddenly drawn to the sound of a snapping branch coming from the woods behind my house. I see a set of eyes again staring at me. *Not this time.* I jump off my hammock and head toward the figure. I try to follow him with my sight as I approach, but by the time I reach the tree line he's gone.

I make my way into the dense preserve, but I can't find him. Several times I look back, ensuring I know how far I am from my house, but it keeps getting smaller in the distance. I pat my pockets for my phone and realize that I left it on the hammock. *Shit.* Okay, if I keep walking in a straight line, I can find my way back. I keep searching for what I am pretty sure is Mr. Wentworth. *If I find him creeping behind my house, so help me, God, I will have his ass arrested, after I beat him.* I turn to look for my house and now I can't see it at all. *Shit, shit, shit! Ok, don't freak out, Katelyn.* I give up my pursuit of Mr. Wentworth and try backtracking. The trees start to all look the same with no clear paths.

"Who are you?"

I whirl around to find the source of the voice. My jaw is clenched and my fists are balled at my sides.

"Erebos?" Without warning, and frighteningly enough, without sound, Erebos is standing in front of me. His gaze is fixed on me and I am pretty sure he isn't even blinking. He is dressed in the same suit he had on earlier.

"What are you doing here?" My eyes dart in every direction, still trying to find a path home.

Erebos steps forward and begins to circle me. The closer he gets, the more my head begins to pound and I am having trouble concentrating. "You are a strong-minded mortal."

Mortal?

"I saw something in you, child." He spits the word child. He continues to circle me and I feel as if my skull is going to crack open. The closer his circle gets around me, the harder it is to breathe, a vortex of sorts is pulling the air from around me. "Will you not defend yourself?" Out of the corner of my eye I see him cock his head at me. "Perhaps, I am wrong about you."

I hear him, but I cannot react to his words. To my right, in the distance I hear leaves crunching. The sound gets closer and closer, but I am now on my knees and I have no idea who is nearby or if I will live to find out. A flash of grey and white light comes from beside me cutting through the vortex, and knocking Erebos out of my line of sight. The ground beneath me begins to spin as I try to take in air, but it's too late, the darkness is here.

My eyes flutter open to the sound of a tea kettle whistling. A tan microfiber sofa and blanket envelop me. A fog clouds my mind and I cannot keep a coherent thought.

"I was wondering if you were going to wake up. You falling into a coma would be pretty difficult to explain to your parents." The familiar voice comes from the next room.

I sit up slowly, taking in my surroundings. The walls around me are a light shade of grey. The house is meticulous with very minimal furniture and no dirt or stains to be seen. The living room isn't very large, but big enough to house the sofa I am on, a loveseat, and a large flat screen tv. Across the hall is an open dining room, and judging from the noises, the kitchen is in the next room.

Mr. Wentworth rounds the corner with a mug in his hands, the steam forming intricate shapes as it rises up.

"How… what?" The only words I can manage to trickle out.

"Oh." He looks at the tea. "It's just the combination of the herbs." He hands me the cup, and though it smells divine, I am afraid of any liquid that can control the shape of its own steam. "Trust me. It will help clear the fog in your head."

How did he know I felt foggy?

I take a sip and almost instantly, I begin to think clearer. "What happened?"

"You don't remember?" He sits on the loveseat, leaning forward, his forearms on his legs and hands clasped

"I remember seeing someone watching me and I thought it was you because I see you a lot. I took off and ran into the woods and there was this guy."

"Do you know who he is?"

"No, well, not really. I'd only met him this afternoon. He said something about seeing something in me, but I don't know what the hell he was talking about." I take another sip of the tea and look at my counselor. "What was he doing to me? When he was walking around me, my head felt like it was going to explode and I couldn't breathe."

He chuckles lowly. "He was trying to get into your mind. But you were somehow able to keep him out. I'm not sure how you were able to do it, being that you are so young and you don't fully have an understanding of your powers yet."

"Wait." I put the mug down on the coffee table. "My what? Did you just say powers?"

He presses his lips together. "Yes."

"Mr. Wentworth, I think you've read too many books, or tried counseling too many kids. There is no such thing as powers." I say, though I, myself am unsure. "You know, I was thinking that maybe I fell and hit my head and imagined all this, but now I wonder if you are the one that has hit his head." I stand, removing the blanket and dropping it on the sofa. "I have to get home. My parents are probably worried."

"Katelyn, I assure you that there is such a thing. What do you think has been happening to you since you were a little girl?"

I stare at him open mouthed. "Those are coincidences, or freak accidents of nature," I half yell, only because I don't know how or why he knows this. "Magic belongs in the books I read! And how did you know that things have been happening since I was a little girl?" I yell at him feeling exposed at the revelation of his knowledge about me.

"There is a lot you don't know, Katelyn. But I can't explain it if you aren't willing to open your mind." He sits with a calm that is unnerving.

"I appreciate you helping me from whatever it was that happened." I open the door and look at him one more time.

He regards me with a sadness now. "When you are willing

to learn the truth, I will be here."

I walk out the door and am suddenly in the woods behind my house. I turn to look at Mr. Wentworth, but he is gone. The entire building has disappeared as if I were never inside of a building at all. I look ahead, a path to my house very clear in my sights. *What the hell just happened?*

As I emerge from the woods I see that the moon is high overhead. *How long was I gone?* I see several people through the windows of the house and one stops at the back door. *Ana.*

She throws open the French doors. "She's here!" she yells as she runs to me, all the people in the house running out behind her.

"Katelyn!" Ana yells as she approaches me and I brace myself for the impact. She throws her arms around me, squeezing me tight. "Are you ok? Where the hell have you been?"

I open my mouth to answer, but my dad comes up right behind her and takes me in a bear hug. "Katie-Kat!" He hasn't called me that since I was about five years old. "Are you alright baby?" He releases me, but takes my face in both his hands turning it every which way, looking for some sign of injury. Beside me, Liz takes my arms and does the same.

"I'm fine," I say, but they continue their inspection. I grab my dad's shoulders. "Daddy!" He stops searching me and looks straight at my eyes. "I'm alright," I say calmly, though calm is the last thing I am right now.

"Where've you been?" His eyes are red and a bit puffy. "We tried calling you and when you wouldn't answer, Liz and I came home, but you weren't here either and when we saw your phone on the hammock, well, we thought-" he pulls me into another bear hug. "We thought you could be hurt or something," he says onto my shoulder before releasing me again.

"I-" I stop and take in their faces, Ana, her parents, Liz and Dad, and two police officers.

"Come on, baby," Liz wraps her arm around my waist, nudging me forward.

I can see everything clearly and though I can think clearly, my memories of what happened seem like a dream.

We get inside and Liz hands me off to my dad who sits me at the kitchen table while she goes to make coffee.

I look again to the police officers and to my dad.

"Kiddo, we were so scared, we were trying to report you as missing, but because it hadn't been twenty-four hours, they couldn't make it official," he tells me, explaining the officers' presence.

"Miss Miller, if you could let us know where you were and what happened?" The taller and slightly rounder of the officers speaks first.

My dad shoots him an annoyed look before looking back

at me. He might be annoyed at them for asking, but I can only imagine that he's just as curious, if not more.

"I was sitting in the hammock this afternoon when I saw someone in the forest behind the house."

"Can you describe the person you saw?" The shorter, thinner officer steps forward, his name badge flashing beneath the kitchen lights. Bell.

"I'm sorry. All I saw from the hammock was two eyes and what I think was a trench coat. The face might have been hooded because I only saw shadows between the trees." I turn my attention to Liz who hands me my favorite mug filled with coffee. "I got off the hammock and started walking into the forest, but the person got farther and farther away, and when I turned to look for the house, I couldn't find my way".

I contemplate whether or not to tell them about Erebos, but I choose to leave him out until I talk to Logan. "I must have fallen and hit my head because I thought I was in a house, and when I got up to walk out the door I was back in the forest and it was dark."

The two officers look at each other. Deputy Bell steps forward and looks me over. "Do you have a welt or lump?"

"No, but my head hurts really bad."

"Could have also been a heat stroke." Deputy Bell says to his partner. "Alright Miss Miller, I think we have all we need. Should you remember anything else, please give us a call.

Your father has my card." He looks at me with a sideways smirk and squinty eyes.

Ana's parents offer to walk the officers out. "Katelyn, if you need anything you and your parents can give us a ring, ok, hon?" I nod as Ana's mom gently squeezes my arm.

Ana slides into the seat next to me and gives me a quick hug. "I'm so glad you're ok. Call or text me later if you are up to it." She smiles before standing and leaves the kitchen and following her parents out the door.

I glance at my phone buzzing on the kitchen table.

"Oh, some guy named Logan has called several times. I answered on the fourth time because we wanted to ask him if he knew where you could be. You might want to call him and let him know you are alright because he seemed very distraught." Liz sits down, raising her eyebrow and I know she's waiting for more information about Logan.

"We met the other day at the library. He just moved to town. He's also the one I was having coffee with the other day." I grab my phone and find six missed calls and texts. I think of the tea as the throbbing in my head begins to finally subside.

"Kate?" His voice sounds desperate and a pang of guilt suddenly hits my stomach as I realize what I have caused everyone.

"Yes."

"Geez, Angel, I've been so worried. Are you ok?"

I wonder how many times I am going to hear that question in the next couple of days.

"Yeah, I'm fine. I'll call you in a bit, I just wanted to let you know I'm alright. Liz told me you called." I glance at Liz and then at my dad who are watching me intently.

"I did, I was worried when I didn't hear back from you. Don't forget though."

"I won't."

I hang up the phone and rub my face with my hands, still trying to process all that happened. I know it wasn't a dream and I know I didn't hit my head, but can I really accept that it was magic?

"So you want to tell us what really happened?"

"What do you mean?" I feign innocence.

"Kiddo, you don't have any bruising or bumps on your head, though I can see that you are in a daze. Are you sure that there isn't something that you just didn't want to tell the police?" He swallows hard and hesitates. "Did something, you know, strange happen?"

"Oh, you mean, did I do something?" I answer sharply as I look down at my hands. The dirt doesn't seem that apparent at first, but then, it's because the shaking draws your attention away from the dried mud.

"You know I didn't mean it like that." He sighs, "Katie, we

know that you don't control those things that happen around you, so I'm not accusing you. I'm just asking if something happened, maybe you got worked up when you saw the stranger, and then…"

My eyes fill with tears and I am about to stop them, but I don't bother. "I don't know exactly what happened, Dad!" I half yell, putting my elbows on the table and burying my face in my hands. "I just … don't know." The tears turn to sobbing and my dad scoots onto the chair next to me, bringing me onto his shoulder.

"It's ok, baby. You're home safe and that's all that matters. We can talk again about it later." He strokes my hair and cuddles me like he did when I was younger.

I wonder to myself why he is always so calm and accepting about the things that happen around me and I pull away for a moment. "I wish I knew why this happens to me."

I cringe as I think of all the little 'events' that have happened that I never told him and Liz about because I was afraid that their understanding would turn to fear or worry.

He doesn't hesitate. He puts his fingers under my chin and lifts my head so that I am looking at him straight in the eye. "Because you are and always have been special. Great and unexplainable things happen around you. That's not necessarily a bad thing."

I sit for a few more minutes in my dad's arms before

heading upstairs to shower. I mull over what my father said and realize for once, that perhaps, I was looking at it wrong. Yes, I can't explain them, but if I could understand it, or what is causing this, I might not feel like a freak. I decide to make it a point to see Mr. Wentworth tomorrow, though I really have no desire to go to school.

I sit on the edge of my bed in my blue and white striped pajama bottoms and cami, my wet hair falling around my face as I lean over onto my knees and stare at my phone, forcing myself to make the call.

"Angel?"

"Hi," is all I can manage.

"Hey." His voice softens and I feel a warmth consume my chest. I'm tempted to ask him to come over and pick me up, just to go for a drive, but after the scare I gave my parents, I think it best to stay home.

"I, I just wanted to hear your voice," I say at almost a whisper as I lay back on my bed.

I hear him sigh. "I've been dying to hear yours. I wanted to go to your house when Liz asked me where you were. I wanted to show up and help them look for you, but she was so distraught that she hung up pretty quickly after I told her that I didn't know where you were." He pauses a moment. "I drove to the coffee shop, I knew your parents probably checked the rink, but I went there anyway as well. I even went down to the beach. I couldn't stand the thought of something happening to you." He sighs again, "What did happen to you?"

I listen to his strong soothing voice and wonder if I should mention Erebos. I don't know what Erebos is to him besides someone he does business with, so maybe not just yet. After I talk with my counselor, I think to myself, and give him the same story I gave to the police and my parents.

"If you saw something like that, why didn't you call someone? Call me?!" He sounds frustrated and I can picture him running his fingers through his hair.

"I guess it's just habit to take care of everything myself. You know?" I turn on my side. "I want to see you tomorrow," I say before I can stop myself.

"Just tell me when and where. Because to be honest, I was going to ask if I could come see you. Right now." His voice gets louder and more excited.

"I don't think I would be good company right now." I look at the glass of water next to my bedside that Liz brought to me after my shower. The white pill next to it should help me sleep, she said.

"You could sit next to me in total silence if you wanted to. I would be fine just being with you."

My stomach twists into knots and a desire to see him pulls at me. *Gosh, what is this effect he has on me?* But I have so much on my mind that I am afraid I will say something before I know what is going on. My head begins to pound once again and I see that the water in the glass begins to spin, forming a vortex.

"No, tomorrow is better."

"Will you tell me the whole story then?" His voice gets softer.

"Maybe." My attention still on the water in the glass that has stopped spinning.

"I'll take it. Goodnight, Angel, sleep well."

"Goodnight, Polo." I hear him laughing at the nickname as we hang up and it brings a much needed smile to my face.

What the hell… I pick up the glass to take the pill but nothing happens to the water. Though I declare myself crazy for the thought, I look at it, trying to will it to move. Nothing, *of course.*

In the morning I convince dad and Liz that I don't need to be watched over and practically have to beg them to go to work. I tell them honestly that I do not want to go to school and they aren't surprised and don't argue. I do mention that I want to talk to my counselor and though they are taken aback, they agree that talking to someone might be a good idea.

I show up at the school, but I don't pull into the parking lot. Instead, I park along the sidewalk by the teacher's parking. Several students walk by and look in and say something to each other almost immediately. I see a black charger with dark windows pull in. Within moments Mr. Wentworth emerges from the vehicle and turns immediately, looking at me. Just like Logan had done the other day. Didn't look around, didn't hesitate, just looked straight at me like he knew I was there. He takes out his phone and makes a call. After a few minutes, he gets back into his car and leaves the parking lot. I am unsure if he wants me to follow him, but I don't really care. I need answers.

He drives to West Beach Park and parks his car, though not near the beach area. He's near the rocky shores that lead to several walking trails and into nearby trees. I pull up three cars down from him and watch first. He exits his car, not bothering to look in my direction, though I know he knows I'm here. He walks over toward the piers and sits on a bench overlooking the ocean.

It takes all the nerve I have, but I get out of the car and head toward him. I feel someone's eyes on me, but when I turn and search the area I don't see anyone, so I continue forward. He never once turns to see if I'm coming. I walk up and sit on the bench beside him.

"Are you ready for the truth?" he asks, his tone low and steady.

CHAPTER 6

I swallow hard. No, I'm probably not ready, but it doesn't matter. I need to know.

"Sort of." *Hey, at least I'm being honest.*

He chuckles and leans forward, resting his elbows on his knees. "First, I need to at least ask if you will be willing to hear me out. Without calling me crazy, without accusing me of anything... nothing of the sort. Can you do that?" He speaks to me while still looking out at the sea.

"Yes," I say, feeling kind of guilty for jumping down his throat yesterday, even though he seemed to be trying to help me.

"To start, I am still doing a bit of research on the man who was in the forest with you yesterday. I may have an idea, but before I let you in on it, I need to be absolutely correct because it can change everything for you."

My eyes widen and I can feel the concern etching itself on my face and soul. Part of me feels like I am stuck in some crazy espionage movie and that this couldn't possibly be real.

"Not that things won't change now, but the severity will be different." He finally looks at me. "What do you know about your mother?"

I open my mouth but the words are stuck in my throat. Of all the things I thought he would ask or talk about, my mother was not in the top five. "I, I know that her name was Catherine. She kept to herself, very much a homebody. She um, she died giving birth to me."

He smirks. "What do you know about that?"

"About her dying at my birth? The doctors said that there was no reason for it. Her heart just stopped."

"I figured as much." He shakes his head.

"Did you know my mother?" My heart leaps into my chest.

"In a way." He sits back, keeping his gaze on me. "What do you know about her family?"

"Just that her family is from England and her family name is Langley." I shrug my shoulders, embarrassed that I do not know more about my mother.

"Hm, then we will skip that for now."

"The 'strange occurrences' that happen around you," he leans forward again, looking for a moment at the ground then back at me, "they have happened when you have been the most emotional, correct?"

I swallow hard and I don't know if the sudden nervousness comes from the fact that things happen around me, or that this man whom I think is a total stranger, knows about them.

"Yes." I breathe as my heart pounds in my ears.

"Since about the age of eight or so, right? Samantha's birthday party?"

I want to jump down his throat again and ask him how he knows about it, but I restrain myself.

"Some girls were bullying her and I was trying to defend her. But she didn't appreciate it. She was letting them bully her because she wanted to be part of their crowd. So, she got mad at me for intervening." I shake my head, unsure of why I am explaining this to him. "She was my best friend and she turned on me. The more worked up I got, the more things began to happen. First it was the wind picking up around us, then the water in the pool bubbling up over the edge and flooding her yard. She-"

"Called you a freak." He finishes for me.

I squint my eyes at him. "How did you know that?"

"I was there." He looks out to the sea. "I've always been

there."

"Wha-, how?"

"Katelyn, to tell you more about who you are, I should probably tell you who I am first."

"I am Gamaliel Wentworth, a Keeper of Balance." He closes his eyes for a moment, "We are a select group of individuals who were put on earth to help keep the peace." He finally looks back to me. "You know how some people are geniuses' and can use more of their brains than others?"

"Yeah."

"Well, there are people who in doing so, can manipulate the energies around them. Energy, as you know, is in everything, especially the elements."

"Wait, are you talking about witches?" I prop my elbow on the back of the bench and turn slightly to face him.

"Some are known by that. As with everything, there are those who use that power for good, and those that use their powers for bad." He lowers his head slightly. "Then there are those that use it to keep the balance between the two. That is me."

"So there are people who are using the elements for bad?"

"Not really. There are people who don't stop at the elements. They assume that because they can control the elements, they should be able to control anything with energy. People included."

I set my jaw and start to wonder why a person would think that it is ok to do that, to mess with people's minds. Then it hits me. Erebos. My expression must have given me away because Mr. Wentworth begins again.

"I see you have just realized that you met one of these people. See, unlike you and the ones who chose evil, my powers go beyond the energy of the elements and general surrounding energies. I suppose you would call it a psychic connection or ability. I know when something is about to happen, or is happening, making it possible for me to intervene if need be to keep the balance. Though that has become increasingly difficult for our kind in recent centuries."

"You can control minds too, can't you? Control people, like the ones you said are evil?"

Mr. Wentworth's lips shoot to the side as he seems to contemplate his answer. "I can. It's not something I like to do, because aside from draining me of my own energy, it simply should not be done."

"But you did it to the officer who went to the school, didn't you? Officer Williams?"

He sighs hard, "I did. I didn't want to, but I did."

"Why?"

"Because explaining to him and the others present what I am explaining to you now, was not an option. Not everyone can deal with the truths of this world."

I shake my head in agreement. *Hell, I'm not sure I can deal with the truths I'm hearing right now!*

"So, going back to what you said before… Why has it become increasingly difficult for your kind to keep the peace lately?" I bite my lip, sorting through the million questions stirring inside of me and picking the ones I think would heed the best information.

"You like to read, yes?" I nod my head.

"Have you ever heard of the Penhale Massacre that occurred in the late 1500's in England?"

"Vaguely. It sounds familiar, but I don't recall the details."

He presses his lips together and thinks a moment before continuing. "The Penhale Massacre was a massacre of an entire family of 'witches' as you call them. In the town of Penhale in England, there were two families. Both born with extraordinary powers. One used its powers for the good of the town, its crops, and trade. The other, well, it used its power to advance themselves in business by manipulating the minds of the ones they dealt with. This went on for a few years without anyone saying anything, but eventually, the other family began to remind them that evil will not prevail, nor go unpunished. Despite the pleas of several family members who had wed and even borne children with the other family, there was a plan set in place to be rid of them before they could stop the growth of their wealth. The names of the two families are

Langley and Blackbourne."

"Langley," I whisper as my heart falls heavily into my stomach.

"Because there were those from the Blackbourne family who opposed the massacre, they tried to warn them, but it was too late. That night, the Blackbournes came down on the Langleys like a force of nature. They started with the mind control, causing some to go mad, thinking that they were hearing from demons. Others were drawn out of the town and murdered, their bodies never to be found. But there was one, Henry Blackbourne who got to a young Langley girl, Abigail Langley, and convinced her to leave with him. They traveled all night until she was so far from the chaos that she would be safe. He then told her that she couldn't go back. She was so distraught at the thought of losing her family that she banished Henry from ever seeing her again, saying that he could have stopped them. But it was not before she vowed revenge on them and put a curse on herself and every other female Langley who would come."

I open my mouth, "So as the phoenix rises from its ashes, so will the White Witch rise from the ashes of her ancestors before her and claim revenge." I cup my hand over my mouth, not understanding where that came from.

"Because of that, every Langley woman will die in childbirth, passing on her powers to her child, keeping the lineage strong until one comes along who is powerful enough to stop the Blackbournes." he finishes, looking at me and furrowing his brow. "Do you understand now? This is why your mother died, and her mother before her, and her mother before her."

I stand from the bench, the enormity of this information settling in my chest. The sounds of the waves crashing hard against the rocks surround me as the sea sprays onto my cheek.

"So I am-" I begin to pace as the waves behind me crash against the rocks harder and harder.

"Yes." Mr. Wentworth stands and reaches out a hand to me, but I cringe away from it. From this man who has forever changed my life.

"I can't take revenge for anyone!" I raise my hands and bring them down bringing a wave so big, it misses the rocks completely and soaks our feet and shoes, for the first time, I realize I caused it and I don't care. "I will not kill someone because of something that happened centuries ago. It's not in me. She was wrong!"

I walk back to the bench, my feet sloshing around in my sneakers, and bury my face in my hands for a moment. I shake my head back and forth trying to take this in, examining myself and wondering how much of this I can handle. I shoot my head back up and stare at Gamaliel, "I'm sorry Mr.

Wentworth… I am sorry that you have wasted your time looking after me in the hopes that I would help you balance this injustice, but I can't."

I look down at my trembling hands and back at my counselor. "I don't think you understand. I can't control the things that happen around me. And I am certainly not a person who can go around hurting other people. Especially for something that happened centuries ago."

Mr. Wentworth stands and I stand with him. "I think that you are the one who does not understand. By now, it is not only about what happened to your family. It is about what can still happen. They know about the curse. They always have. They have killed many of my kind in order to keep themselves in hiding, changing their names, moving, waiting for the day that they can eliminate their last threat."

"I… I don't think I can listen to any more of this. Not now." The sea beside us has calmed slightly, but still it crashes onto the rocks harder than it should considering there is no wind.

"I know this is a lot and when you are ready, we can talk again."

"Aren't there other … other witches, or guy witches, or wizards, or whatever they are called who can help?"

"No. Well, yes, there are others, but no family has ever been able to collectively amount the power that the Langleys and Blackbournes did." He looks at me with his brows pinched as his eyes search my face for a reaction.

"What if I don't want to do this? What if I can't hurt anyone?" I say lowly pressing my feet into the soles of my shoes and watching the water bubbles pour out the sides.

"I cannot push you to do anything you do not want to do."

Unable to process any more, I begin to walk back to my car, when I hear him shout after me. "I am not the only one who will know who you are. They will figure it out. Those with an understanding of magic can feel the energies of other magical beings and your energy grows stronger by the day. They will come for you, they will come for your family. They always do."

I stop in my tracks and wonder if he is right, but convince myself that it has been so long that maybe, just maybe, it has been so long, they have forgotten.

"Hello?"

I listen to his voice for a moment and realize that I don't even remember pressing the icon to call him, like it was more of an instinct and desire than a conscious act.

"Angel? Are you there?"

My breath hitches as I try to stop the tears from rolling down my face. I realize I can't stop them and pull over to the side of the road, feeling the breakdown coming on. That horrible feeling that I hadn't experienced since I was little; The clamping in my chest pulling on every emotion so tight that they have no choice but to bend to the will of the pain. My breathing comes harder and despite my desire to speak, I can't, not without giving in.

"I can hear you, Kate. Are you alright?" I hear the pleading and concern in his voice and suddenly I know why I called him.

"No." I manage before the tears stream down my face. As I talk to him I realize that maybe Erebos is lurking around Logan because of me. *What if Mr. Wentworth is right, what if the people around me are in danger?* "Logan, we need to meet. I need to talk to you."

"What's going on?"

I can hear the desperation in Logan's voice. "I'll tell you when I see you. Meet me at my house. I'll text you the address so you can put it in your GPS."

"Ang-"

I cut him off and text him the address quickly before wiping my face and shifting back into drive. I look around and wonder what I can tell Dad and Liz. What would they think if I told them everything Mr. Wentworth said. I run several scenarios in my head on the way home with not one ending positively. Not sure there are many parents who want to know that their kid is a witch who is supposed to carry out a curse or prophesy or whatever and kill someone.

I find myself pacing my living room and looking out the window every five minutes waiting for the black SUV to pull in, so naturally it's when I decide to go make coffee that he arrives. Dammit! The doorbell echoes through the house as I wipe coffee grounds off the counter that I flung from surprise. I toss what's left in my hands into the sink and abandon my coffee desire. For now.

When I open the door, I am hit by the gorgeous sight in front of me. Logan's wavy hair is combed back and held down with a bit of gel. He's dressed again in a fitted button down shirt and dress pants, though this time, the shirt is a royal blue that makes his eyes pop. His brows are pinched as he studies my face, but one corner of his mouth still manages to rise. "Hi Angel."

Though my chest is heavy and my mind is swirling I manage a smile as I step out of the way for Logan to ease into the foyer. As I close the door, he steps behind me, putting his hands on my shoulders. I take a jagged breath and turn around. His hand slides from my shoulder to my cheek. I open my mouth to say something, but instead I step forward, wrapping my arms around his waist and laying my head on his chest. At first his chin rests on my head, but then I feel his cheek on me as he tightens his grip. I allow my mind to wander and question whether or not it's normal to be falling this fast for someone I just met, especially when I am so used to easily pushing everyone away. The word normal resonates in my mind and I see that even matters of the heart are not normal when it comes to me.

Logan rubs one hand along my back as the other sits entwined in my hair at the base of head. My thoughts are not as rampant as they had been before he got here and I decide that I could be here all day with him.

"Katelyn." He lifts his cheek from my head and I pull back to look at him, reluctantly softening my hold on him. "I won't ask the obvious question since I know the answer; you are not ok, so I will simply ask this... Will you tell me what is going on?"

I purse my lips together and nod as I take him by the hand and lead him to the living room. I sigh as I wonder just how much I can tell him. I mean sure, he cares about me, and I can't stop thinking about him, and every time I see him I want to throw myself into his arms, but what do I really know about him? How much can I say to him before he runs screaming for the hills?

He sits down next to me, leaning forward on his elbows. I see his hand twitch a couple of times and I think it's because he wants to hold my hand again, but decides not to. "You're deciding how much you should tell me."

My eyes widen as I look at him. "How did…"

"It's not that hard to see." He clasps his hands. "Start with why you called me this afternoon." He smiles at me and my heart beats faster. "Maybe that will make it easier."

I sigh and sit up straight, my own fingers laced in my lap. "I found out something today."

"Okay." Logan sits up, his eyes fixed on me and his brow is pinched again.

I shake my head. "I can't believe I thought I could tell you this without you thinking that I am crazy." I stand and walk to the fireplace across the room, taking a picture of my mom off the mantle and running my finger over it before putting it back.

Logan pushes himself off the sofa, "I am not going to think you are crazy." He walks over, taking my hand in his. He glances at the picture I was holding. "Is that you with your mom? Well, technically, inside your mom…"

I nod. "Yeah, my dad said that he took that the day before she gave birth to me."

I take a deep breath as I put the picture back and look at him. "I think you might be in trouble," I blurt out.

"What?" Logan steps back locking his gaze with mine. "Why would you think that?"

I bite the corner of my lip for a moment before answering, "Because of me."

I think that he is about to distance himself from me, but instead he laces his fingers with mine. "What on earth makes you think that you've gotten me in trouble?" He thinks for a minute. "Oh, if this about the meeting that my mother called me about when we were-"

I shake my head. "I didn't mean trouble, I meant danger. And it has nothing to do with the conversation with your mom."

"Does it have to do with you disappearing?"

"Somewhat." I let go of his hand and walk across the room, sitting on the window seat, burying my face in my hand. "ARGH! Why is this so hard?!" I stand again as he is walking toward me. "I don't know what it is about you, Logan, but you make me so comfortable with you that I want to tell you everything about me, good and bad."

"Is that a bad thing, because you have that effect on me too?"

"No, it's not a bad thing, but there are things that I... that happen to... I mean around..." I stop and take a deep breath, realizing that my rambling isn't going to get my anywhere. "Alright, let's start with my disappearance."

Logan stays a few feet away from me and slides his hands in his pockets as he pushes his lips out a moment. "Alright."

"What I told you was true. It wasn't the whole truth, but it was true. I did see someone looking at me and I did go into the woods. But once I was there, something strange happened."

I stop and try to gauge his reaction but he is only looking at me curiously and with sadness. I continue anyway. "Though I have been in those woods a hundred times over, I lost sight of my house, as if by magic and here is where it gets crazy…. I thought I saw Erebos."

Logan's jaw clenched.

"I don't know if he was really there, or if I just hallucinated the whole thing, but he was walking around me, saying something like he thought he saw something in me, or I'm not who he thought I was and at the same time, my head was pounding something awful and I could barely breathe." I continued recounting the story up to the part where I returned home. I rub my face with my hands. "Saying it out loud just makes it sound even crazier and I don't know why I felt I needed to tell you, but I have a feeling that someone might be after me for reasons I can't explain yet. If they are, I don't want you to be hurt because of me. I know we just met, but I couldn't bear that, Logan." My eyes welled up with tears as I look straight at two blue pools. "I just couldn't," I finish, my voice breaking slightly.

Logan steps forward grabbing my face and pressing his forehead to mine. "Nothing is going to happen to me and nothing is going to happen to you. Do you understand me, Angel? Nothing." His breath is hot on my face and lips are so close to mine I can almost feel them.

I nod my head as he wipes my tears away with his thumbs.

His jaw is set and his eyes bore into mine without a hint of a smile. "I need to know, are you sure you saw Erebos?"

"Not one hundred percent. I mean, to be honest, it all looked like a dream, but I know it wasn't!" I raise my voice at the end as I move my head to be eye to eye with him. "I just... I can't prove it. It may very well be someone else. I don't want you confronting him only to find out I have finally lost my mind."

"And you can't tell me anything else?"

I bite the corner of my lip as the word freak flashes before my eyes. "No." I look down at my feet as he pulls me to him, the rhythm of his heart pounding in my ears.

"You know, nothing you can say will change how I feel about you." He places a kiss on the top of my head. "Look, Kate, I know I said on that first day that I want to be your friend, but I would be lying if I said I didn't feel more than that. I swear I'm not trying to push you, but I think you should know that."

I nod my affirmation, not taking my head off his chest, finding a new place I now feel safe.

"Just keep an eye out. Please." I speak onto his chest and

the silence that follows is blissful. A calm I have not had in years comes over me while I am wrapped in his arms.

After what must be at least been five or ten minutes I let go of him. "How do you do that?"

"What?" Logan looks at me, his eyebrows knitted close together in thought.

I smile for the first time today. "Nothing... nothing at all." Just then my phone buzzes in my pocket.

Dad - Just checking in on you and letting you know we will have to be here 'til late.

I text back, letting him know that I am alright and that a day off has done me good.

Logan smiles at me as I pocket my phone. "Alright, so now that you are smiling again, I have to go take care of something. Promise me that I can see you again later?"

I nod, though I want to ask him not to go.

Logan kisses me on the forehead and walks to the door. "I'll text you later."

I lock the door behind him and pass the living room heading back to the kitchen. I feel that a small amount of the weight on my shoulders has been lifted. I look around and assess the mess I made before Logan had gotten here, the only mess in my step-mother's immaculate kitchen, that she designed herself. The tan walls and white trim bringing out the most beautiful tone of the dark oak cabinets, her granite countertops glimmering beneath the lights. Well, all but the area that was still covered in coffee grounds.

I push the coffee maker back against the tile backsplash, put my mug back in the cabinet and reach for some paper towels. I open the faucet and before I can get the towel to the water, it splashes forward, dousing the napkin. I slam the faucet closed as I stare at the napkin in my hand. "That didn't just happen." I wring out the paper towel and unable to help myself, I stare at the water dripping into the sink, willing it to do something.

Nothing.

"Maybe I need to be more specific," I say out loud to myself. I clean up most of the coffee grounds and put the paper towel in the trash. I grab another and hesitate for a moment before opening the faucet again.

"Go." Nothing.

"Splash," I say, trying to command the water to move. Nothing.

I'm talking to water… this can't possibly be a good thing.

I watch as the water is running, I place my hand at the other end of the sink, and picture the water doing what it did before. No words, just picturing the water. No sooner did the thought begin, did the water splash forward again. I slam the faucet shut again and put my free hand over my mouth. I think of the waves pounding the rocks at the beach, and the vortex in the cup the other night and realize I have finally controlled one of these 'events'.

My heart is beating so hard I feel like it's going to burst. I feel the adrenaline running through me, or could that be something else? No, I cannot think like that. One step at a time. I wring the paper towel again and clean up the remaining grounds.

As soon as I toss the paper into the trash my mind begins to wander to the things that Mr. Wentworth had told me. *Power over elements*. Considering that up until now I hadn't had great luck with water, I was secretly grateful for never having been around any flames when I was very emotional. Suddenly, the first night at the coffee shop with Logan comes to mind. My emotions running high and the unforeseen wind storm that formed outside. I walk over to the window and pull the flowery curtains to the side. No wind.

"OK, maybe I'm blowing this out of proportion. If, and that is a big if, I do have any powers, it doesn't mean that I have *the* powers that the favorite, or chosen one or whatever that witch will be called will have." By now I am pacing the kitchen as I talk out loud to myself, happy that no one is around to witness it. I am tempted to skate tonight to see if I can see the ice flurries again and wonder how I would even make that happen. *If* I could make that happen.

My head starts to hurt as all these thoughts bombard me at once, as well as the entire conversation from this morning and my conversation with Logan. I would have to say that it seems even more surreal than my conversation with Mr. Wentworth. I have never confided in anyone like that, let alone allow them to see me so vulnerable, but with Logan I couldn't help myself. I want to keep my walls up around him, but I can't. I walk into the living room and throw myself on the sofa in the hopes that with some rest, my headache will subside.

The heavy pounding on the door yanks me from the deep sleep. I reach for my phone that has fallen on the floor. Six forty two, two missed calls and six texts. I sit up quickly and rub my face. *Holy crap, I slept the entire afternoon*, I push myself off the sofa and walk to the door, scanning my phone as the pounding continues. One text from my dad, letting me know he is taking Liz out to dinner and asking me to text back if I want to go, and the others are from Logan. I gaze through the peep hole and smile at the mess of dark hair in front of it. I don't bother reading the messages and instead open the door to find Logan leaning with one arm against the door frame, his gaze seemingly on the ground as he sighs hard. "I was starting to worry." He lifts his head slowly and his light blue eyes have darkened beneath his pinched eyebrows. Concern etched in his gaze. My attention is immediately drawn to the red area along his jaw.

"What happened?" I grab his hand and as he stands straight, I see that his shirt is slightly untucked and there are marks on the front where someone clearly grabbed him. "Logan, what the-"

"I'm fine." He interrupts, faking a smile.

I usher him in and walk him to the sofa. "I just got your texts and calls, I am so sorry. I took a nap to get rid of a headache and ended up sleeping the entire afternoon. I've never done that." He puts his hand to my face and I push into his palm.

"It's ok. I'm just glad you are alright." He presses his forehead to mine.

My gosh, I love when he does that.

"What happened to you?" I whisper as I bring my eyes up to meet his gaze, drawing my lips dangerously close to his. He has both his hands on my face and I see his lips curl up as he just stares at me.

"I tracked down Erebos and had a chat with him." He licks his lips and I can smell the mint on his breath. "I didn't want to outright accuse him of showing up at your house since you weren't one hundred percent sure. So I asked him if he had seen you. He hesitated when he answered." Logan gives a wicked smirk and raises an eyebrow. "Bad move. I didn't bother to ask him again. Instead I explained that he is never to come near you again, or he will deal with me."

Logan releases my face and takes my hands in his. "He didn't appreciate me threatening him."

"So he hit you? For someone who does business with you, he sure has no idea how to behave!" I clench my teeth as I bring my hand up to his bruising jaw bone, caressing it carefully.

"Well, Erebos is also family, so he thinks he can do or say as he pleases."

"Oh." I close my eyes for a moment. "Dammit, I didn't mean to cause problems in your family." My gut twists.

"What? What are you apologizing for? It's not your fault that he looked for you."

I sigh. "Speaking of that," I shuffle my feet, "why do you suppose he did? Did he say?"

Logan set his jaw, his gaze distant. "No. He is a little psychotic with the handling of business and might have thought you were a threat or something."

"A threat?" I set my hands on my hips. "How would I be a threat?"

Logan takes my hands off my hips and laces his fingers with mine, a sweet smile makes its way across his face. "Because you have distracted me since I met you." He yanks me close until I am against him, letting go of my hands as he wraps his arms around me. "The last thing I have wanted to think about is business." He licks his lips again and I am more than tempted to push up on the balls of my feet and press my lips to his, but I refrain.

"Watch it, Polo, you don't want to get too close. I'm a loner, remember? What if I decide to push you away again?" I give him a sly grin.

"I will push back harder to get close to you again." He brings his face down until his nose meets mine.

Of course! I think as the phone at his hip buzzes, though he doesn't seem as phased as I am. "Don't you have to get that?"

"I'd rather not." He smiles wide until it reaches his eyes, but the buzzing doesn't stop. He sighs and resigns himself to unclipping the phone and sliding it open. "Hey." I vaguely hear a woman's voice, but I can't make out the words. "Yeah, I did."

Logan takes a step back and his lips are pressed into a thin line. "I tried asking nicely and it didn't work." He starts pacing the length of the living room, reaching the window seat at the far end. "Because she is important to me." I hear him say as he walks back to me. "No," he rolls his eyes. "Why?" He rolls his eyes. "Fine… fine, I'll think about it. Bye." Logan clips the phone back onto the holster.

"Everything ok?" I dig my hands into my pockets.

Logan looks me over and a corner of his mouth creeps up. "It seems that I may have called a bit of unwanted attention to us." He walks closer and puts his hands on my hips, his fingers grazing the skin I exposed when I pushed my hands into my pockets. A shiver runs through me and I feel a wicked smile creep across my face.

"Us?" I question, raising my eyebrow.

He purses his lips together then lets out a quick laugh. "Yes, us. My mother heard about me confronting Erebos."

"Oh."

"See, I've never been this... distracted with anyone and have never defended someone to anyone in my family."

"You're kidding, right?" I raise an eyebrow again. "You've never had a girlfr-..." I stop myself unwilling to say the word because I am not sure if that is what I am. "A girl you were seeing that you really liked, or fell for, or were distracted by? I find that really hard to believe, Polo."

"Why is that?" He releases me and steps back. "Why do you keep finding that so hard to believe? You said the same thing at the coffee shop."

"Because!" I pull my hands out of my pocket and point them in his direction. "Look at you! I don't even know why you are here!"

"What?" Logan's expression drops.

"No, not like that." I drop my face in my hands for a

moment and look at him again. "I mean… you can have any girl you want. I'm not saying I'm ugly, but I know there are prettier girls out there with better bodies who would kill for a chance to be with you. And you chose me, a girl who lately crazy shit has been happening around… and to! A girl, who looks more like the girl next door than a girl in a magazine. A girl who has a little more hips that half the girls in Shippan. A girl who pushes everyone away and responds with a sarcastic comment for half the stuff people say to her. A girl who…"

"Who cares more than she likes to let on," he interrupts as he studies me, his eyes a little lighter blue than when he got here. "A girl, whose reason for pushing people away is probably because she doesn't want to get hurt. A girl, who if I had the choice *would* be in a magazine because I say she is gorgeous. A girl who," he steps forward putting his hands on my hips again, sending a warmth throughout my body. "yes, does not look like she starves herself, but damned if you don't look like you are one hell of an athlete." He runs his hands up to my waist, his thumbs grazing my stomach again. "I don't want any of those other girls." The corners of his lips pull up. "I don't care who they are or what they think they can offer. I can guarantee that none of them can have the effect you have on me."

"You sure about that, Polo?" I cross my hands over my chest beneath slightly above average breasts. "I can be a pretty big pain in the ass."

"Oh, I know that." His expression lightens and he lets go of my hips as he folds his arms too, stretching his dress shirt tight against the muscles in his arms and chest.

"Oh really?!" I drop my hands to my hips trying to feign anger, but his response was not what I expected and I really just want to laugh.

"Yes, really. But I like a challenge." He furrows his brow and cocks his head to the side. "I thought you would have figured that out by now… hhmmm, maybe you are a bigger challenge than I thought."

I gasp with exaggeration and smack him playfully on his arm, feeling the firmness of his biceps first hands. *Damn.* Logan drops his hands and quickly closes the gap between us, but I step back out of reach. "Wouldn't want to make it too easy for you." I say as I cock my head to the side and raise my eyebrow at him again.

Logan smiles big and nods.

I open my mouth to say something but shut it quickly and turn to walk to the kitchen. "Would you like something to drink?" I call over my shoulder.

Logan follows behind and settles into a chair that he pulls out from under the breakfast table. "Can I ask you something?" he starts as I grab a glass and walk to the refrigerator.

"Sure."

"Were you about to say something right before coming over here?" He shrugs his shoulders and runs a hand through his hair. "It just looked like you were going to say something to me, but didn't."

"I was." I press the glass to the lever on the fridge and fill it with water before turning around again. "I just... "I chew on my lip wondering if I should bring down another wall but decide to wait.

As I hand him the glass I see that the water inside is swirling hard and it almost slips from my hand. Logan puts out both his hands, steadying mine and the glass. "You ok?"

"Yeah." I look down at the water that has slowed and then back to him. "I wanted to ask you something, but I think I'll wait."

Logan furrows his brows. "You sure about that? You can ask me anything you want."

I tuck a lock of hair behind my ear. "I know," I say, though I didn't actually know that. I wonder if I should let him in more than I already have and decide against it, yet again. As it is, I'm not sure just how dangerous it could be for him.

CHAPTER 7

It's Friday morning and the week has gone by pretty quickly, miraculously, without drama or 'occurrences'. I spend almost every night with Logan either at the coffee shop or sitting in my hammock in the backyard. Dad and Liz seem to like him. Tuesday night they had gotten home from working late to find Logan and I sitting on the sofa watching a movie, dad was a bit stand-off-ish, in his attempt to do 'the dad thing' as he called it. It was actually quite amusing.

I pull my black vintage rockabilly Audrey Hepburn style dress from the closet and sigh. Graduation day. As I slip it on and zip up the back, I can't help but think of the relief today brings. Finally putting an end to the torturous past four years will allow me to concentrate on other things. Not like I haven't already been doing that, though. I have done endless research on the Penhale Massacre. I am disappointed to find there hasn't been much information put out on it. I am definitely feeling much more relaxed around Mr. Wentworth and although I feel a pull to talk to him some more, I still don't feel like I'm ready.

I put on my five inch black heels with a satin bow at the back of the ankle strap and run my hands over my just straightened hair. I look in the mirror and drag my fingers along the small belt at my waist. With my hair straightened like this, I look a little less like my mother and I'm not sure I like it.

My mother, I think of her and my thoughts wander to whether or not she struggled with her powers as I do. According to my father she was raised by her aunt after her mother died giving birth to her, but I have no idea if our 'powers' manifest in each of us, or just some. I only met this aunt once when I was much younger and I hear from her through cards on my birthday and Christmas. I briefly entertain the thought of looking up this one connection to my mother's past to find out more about her and make a mental note to consider it seriously later. I was wondering again last night whether or not I should say anything to Logan when he was over, but chickened out again.

"What's wrong?" Logan shifts to be closer to me as the hammock swings in the breeze, his watch catching the glimmer of light from the night sky.

"Nothing." I turn my attention away, looking for constellations. Too bad I only know three of them.

"That's what you always say." He drags a lock of hair that the wind has blown over across my neck back onto the hammock. A shiver to run through me as his finger touches my skin.

"Maybe that's always the case." I shrug my shoulders, while keeping my attention on the stars.

"Or maybe you're hiding something from me."

I close my eyes when his two fingers touch my chin, turning my face to him.

"I might surprise you, I'm not like other guys you know. Or other people for that matter." He smiles and I catch the reflection of a few stars in his eyes as the wind softly blows his hair about.

I can't stop the smile creeping across my face, not that I want to, honestly. "I know you're not. You don't take no for an answer and you apparently favor socially awkward freakish girls."

"And there it is." Logan rolls his eyes and leans back on the hammock.

"There what is?" I prop myself on my elbow and pinch my brow.

"The self-deprecating remark that you always throw out when you don't want to answer, or are unsure of what to say." He puts his arms *up, resting his hands behind his head and pulling his shirt up just high enough to expose some of his amazing abs.*

"I...I'm sorry. Just habit I guess." I force myself to get closer to him this time, leaning on his chest and dragging my hand along the hem of his shirt just so my fingers can touch his tight skin, causing him to sigh. Which is sweet, or torturous since I know that it might be too soon to go any further.

"I know." He kisses the top of my head and brings one arm down to wrap around me. I drag my hand up to rest on his chest. "I just wish you could see yourself, the way I do."

A soft knock on my door pulls me from my thoughts. "Kate?" My dad's voice comes through.

"Come in."

My dad walks in but stops a foot into the doorway. "Wow." He chews on the inside of his lip. "So much for being my little girl." he huffs.

I smile at my dad. "I'm always going to be your little girl. Isn't that what you've said?"

My dad laughs and steps in closer. "Yes, I have." He looks down at a box in his hands. "Liz and I got you something." He holds out the black box with a white satin bow.

"Dad, you didn't-"

He holds up his hand stopping me. "Yes, we did. Happy Graduation Day." He gives me a crooked smile.

I pull the white ribbon, undoing the bow and open up the box. Inside hangs a delicate platinum necklace with a heart shaped diamond studded locket. The round diamonds trace the intertwining hearts and fleur-de-lis patterns. "Oh dad, you guys really-"

"Open it." he says softly.

I open the locket to find my dad's family crest is on one side and my mother's is on the other. On the back it's engraved: *Always in your heart as you are in ours*.

I throw my arms around my dad as tears roll down my face. His Irish Spring soap smell surrounds me and I squeeze harder.

"I figured that pictures might be kind of cheesy so, I went with the crests." He says as he lets me go.

"It's perfect." I unlock the clasp and bring it up around my neck. The perfect accessory to my black dress. I wipe the tears from my face and check my make-up to make sure that I didn't ruin it. My pretty decent attempt at a light smoky eye look is still intact and I can't stop looking at my new locket. Liz walks into the room and I run over to her, throwing my arms around her neck. "Thank you so much, Liz!"

"Aw, you are so very welcome. We just wanted to let you know how proud we are of you." Liz lets me go, but grabs hold of my hands. "So," she gives a smirk and raises her eyebrow, "will Logan be at the graduation?"

I blush a little and steal a glance at my dad. "Yeah. He is going to meet us there and then he said he has something planned for me this evening."

"I like him." Liz winks at me and lets go of my hands. "He's brought out a side of you that we were afraid we would never get a chance to see."

My dad shakes his head. "He'd just better not break my girl's heart. That's all I'm saying." My dad takes Liz's hand and starts heading out of the room. "Oh, I forgot, there is one more gift. Now, this is a birthday, graduation, acceptance into University gift rolled into one. Okay?"

I scrunch my nose at my dad as he reaches into his pocket, pulls something out and tosses it at me. I put out my hand to catch it and the metal clinks against the white gold ring my dad gave to me on my sixteenth birthday. I open my hand to see a brand new key hooked onto a phoenix keychain that reads: Kate's Jeep.

My mouth drops open and I stare at my dad and Liz. Their smiles are so wide they reach their eyes.

"You're kidding!" I scream excitedly.

My dad lets out a chuckle. "Go find out for yourself."

I stomp my feet like a child for a minute and run out the doorway right past them and down the stairs, trying not to twist my ankle in the process. Heels and stairs are not a good mix!

I yank open the front door and sitting in the driveway is a brand new twenty-fourteen black Jeep Wrangler Unlimited with all the grills and bars, extra-large tires, and a big red bow on the top of it. "Holy Crap! I can't believe you guys did this!" I turn to find my dad and Liz right behind me. I throw my arms around them and squeeze them tight. "Is this what you were doing this morning?"

They look at each other with a sideways glance and laugh.

I run out to my new car and immediately upon opening the door I am hit with the new car smell that I thought I would never experience for myself. I sit in the driver's seat and take in all the accessories and buttons and black leather accents.

"Turn it on!" My dad yells out as he approaches the driver door.

I slide the key into the ignition and turn, reveling in the roar of the engine, still unable to believe that it is mine. I hug the steering wheel before turning it off and locking it up. "This must have cost you-"

"Ah!" My dad puts up his hand. "Don't go there."

I bite the inside of my lip and hug them again. "Thank you so much, guys!"

I go inside to get my purse, cap and gown, and before leaving I text a picture of my new Jeep to Logan.

My parents decide to go in a separate car to the graduation since they have to go to the rink for a bit afterwards. I excitedly get into my new jeep and touch every inch of this SUV that I can reach while I am driving to the country club that has agreed to host our graduation.

I pull into a parking spot near the entrance with my parents pulling into the spot right beside me. I put on my gown, though I haven't zipped it up, and I keep my cap in my hands with my clutch that is hanging off my wrist. I glance at the rolling golf greens that must have been freshly cut this morning since the scent of cut grass is the first to hit my senses when I step out.

We make our way to the main hall and a mob of parents and their children are already crowding the front. I pass Samantha and her goons and they only glance at me for a second before turning their attention back to the fountain just in front of the main doors. As I approach the crowd of students near the main doors, I see that there are several girls looking in that direction and I wonder if someone's celebrity parent or sibling is attending the graduation.

I try to find the celebrity they are all gawking at and I see Logan standing by the fountain. His hair is combed back with a couple of waves that have fallen near his temples, he shaved the scruff he had yesterday, so the sun is practically gleaming off his chiseled jawline. He's in his fitted slacks, with a thin striped maroon and black dress shirt and a black vest over it. If I didn't know better, I would say that the entire suit was tailored to fit him so snugly.

He spots me through the crowd and smiles as some girls nearby giggle and begin to argue over which one of them he was smiling at. While I get closer, I realize that the person they were all staring at was Logan.

He takes a few steps to meet me and stops just inches from my face, his hand wrapping around my waist as he plants a soft kiss on my cheek and hands me a dozen dark red roses. "You look absolutely stunning." I feel myself blushing, but I do not pull away. He wraps his arms tight around me and I see several girls whispering amongst themselves and shaking their heads. *Guess the freak didn't do too bad, huh?*

My parents walk up behind me and Logan hugs Liz and shakes my dad's hand.

"Logan, why don't you sit with us?" My dad offers, and a warmth consumes me.

"It would be my pleasure, sir."

Logan takes my hand and we walk in until I'm told that I have to go to another room to prepare for the class entrance.

The entire graduation barely takes more than an hour. Our class is pretty small in comparison to other high schools due to the extremely selective process of which kids can attend, as well as the cost. Several girls that I rarely talk to lean over and said hello, sure to ask if my boyfriend is an actor. Ana, who is sitting next to me and I giggle over the newly found interest in getting to know me and my life.

"So, Ms. Graduate. What will you be doing now?" Logan takes my hand as we are walking out about an hour later and plants a kiss on top of it.

Before I could answer, my dad picks up his pace, stepping up beside Logan. "Actually Logan, we wanted to take Katelyn out to lunch and would like to ask you to join us."

For a moment, I felt like one of those cartoons whose mouth actually hits the ground when something shocking happens.

"Are… Are you sure, Mr. Miller, I would hate to intrude." I smile at Logan's charm and refinement, so rarely found in guys his age.

"You would not be intruding and please, call me Rick."

From behind my dad Liz is beaming a smile at me and I have a funny feeling that she had a lot to do with him opening up like this.

"I would love to, then. Thank you." Logan reaches out and shakes my dad's hand.

Dad and Liz get into their car, leaving Logan and I to sort out transportation. Knowing how excited I am about my new car, Logan offers to leave his car here and either pick it up later, or have someone pick it up, and go in my car.

"So are you going to tell me what the plan is for tonight?" I ask with my voice a little softer than usual in the hopes that he will cave.

"No chance. You will just have to be surprised." He reaches over and grabs my hand, bringing it up over for another kiss. I thank God that we are at a red light because I watch his lips as they touch my hand and wish they were touching my lips. So many times we had been so close and either he would decide otherwise or we would be interrupted.

"Well, if I don't know, then how will I know what the dress code is?" I try once again to get it out of him.

"Nice try, but to be honest, what you have on now is perfect."

The afternoon goes by smoothly at a restaurant on the ocean that my dad chose. At one point the waitress points out that the waves are pounding the rocks below us are much stronger than they should be considering the wind is so mild. Immediately Liz looks at me and smiles. I had told Liz about the fact that it seemed all the 'occurrences' happen when there are high emotions going on. I even recalled that when my father first told me the story of the night my mother died, a storm rolled in and lasted all night and the next day.

I looked at the incoming waves and realized that the waitress was right. I take a deep breath and close my eyes for a moment breathing in the calm, though I am really just excited about how well the day is going and I am anxious about the surprise tonight.

As we are finishing up desert, my dad and Liz tell Logan all about the competition tomorrow and Sunday and how they will be very busy. Logan of course is the first to volunteer to keep an eye on me.

As we pull out of the restaurant and watch my parents drive off to the rink, a calm settles over me. "Alright, Mr. Blackwell, where would you like me to drive you to?" I ask in my best British accent.

Logan chuckles loudly, "Actually, I wanted to ask something of you."

I stop at the exit of the restaurant parking lot and look at him. "What is it?"

"I thought maybe we can go by my house. My mom is there, and well…" He drops his gaze and brings it back to me. "The more time I spend with you, the more she asks about meeting you."

I bite the inside of my lip as a nervous weight drops in my stomach. *His Mom? He wants me to meet his mom?* I open my mouth to say something but nothing comes out.

"We don't have to, if you don't want-"

"I'd love to," I cut him off, though I'm pretty sure that was an exaggeration. "But if that's the case, then we should just go get your car at the country club and take it back to your place." I say as my heart beats triple in my ears.

I follow Logan all the way down the roads of what looks

to be the richest neighborhoods I've ever seen. As we drive past the Stamford Yacht Club I begin to wonder how much farther we will be driving since I can already see the ocean from here.

Large hedges and iron gates hinged to stone pillars surround the driveway he pulls into. As he pulls up to the gates, he punches a code into a small box and the iron gates begin to creak open. The knots in my stomach get bigger and I begin to get nauseous. If someone had told me last weekend that I would be dating someone I probably would have laughed in their face, yet, here I am meeting his mom. I flip the visor down and check my make up quickly before approaching the house.

The road winds through several groups of trees before opening up to a fountain and a beautiful old Victorian style home that would normally be seen in a movie or some TV show about celebrity homes. The outside is made with tan colored stones, with several pillars lining the front porch. *Do they even call it a porch when it's that big?* There are meticulously trimmed bushes surrounding the walls and lining pathways leading out to the sides of the house. It has a very castle-esque feeling to it, and looks like something you might find in the English countryside.

Logan passes the front entrance and pulls off to the side where there are easily six parking spaces, two of which are occupied by the newest model Mercedes and Cadillac SUV. *Oh man, what have I gotten myself into?* I turn off the Jeep and reach for my clutch to find my hands shaking. *Calm down, Kate, you've got this. You can meet his mom, be nice, and keep your sarcastic tone to a minimum.*

My door swings open and Logan puts out his hand. "Are you sure you're okay with this? We can leave right now."

I smile at him and take his hands. "More than okay." I lie.

The smell of the sea mixed with the scent of the surrounding rose bushes and lilacs envelop me as I slide out of the car. The size and colors of the flowers amaze me and there is not one rose that is any smaller than my fist. Each one is beautifully open and calling to the sun for its warmth.

The sound of the pounding waves in the distance and overhead clouds remind me to keep my emotions under control. I take a deep breath and make my way with Logan to the large wooden double doors with ironwork twisting all around them and the small windows they house. Before Logan can even insert his key, the doors begin to open.

A tall balding man, with white hair along the sides of his head stands at the entrance. His dress shoes quickly pick up the glare of the sun proving that they have been shined to a T. His slacks are very neatly pressed, as well as his black vest and white shirt. He has a plain grey tie around his neck, neatly tucked into the vest.

A butler? Seriously? He has a butler? Oh man, I am way out of my element here.

"Good afternoon, Mister Blackwell," his voice is kind, almost grandfatherly.

"Good afternoon, Harrison. This is my girlfriend, Katelyn Miller." Logan flashes a smile at me and winks.

Girlfriend? Okay, I knew we were headed that way, but I didn't know that he considered me like that already. I feel a blush consume my body.

"Good afternoon, Miss Miller. It is a pleasure." Harrison inclines his head to me.

"Thank you, the pleasure is mine, and please call me Katelyn."

"Yes, Miss Katelyn." He smiles at me as we walk in.

As we enter, the first thing I see is a table in the center with a huge arrangement of flowers in beautiful summer colors. To the right and left of the entryway are staircases that start off wide, and get more narrow as they reach the top to convene at a beautiful second floor balcony. The dark wood floors all around the house bring out the colors in every piece of furniture and every wall. To the right of me, I see a sitting room with several chairs, sofas, and various coffee and end tables. To the left, I find a beautiful mahogany table that looks easily as if it were plucked directly from the Victorian era, with various carvings and matching chairs. A large stone fireplace takes up the back wall behind it.

From a doorway behind the right staircase emerges a beautiful woman. She seems no taller than five foot five or six, with straight black hair that curls at the end. Her skin is flawless, save for a few laugh lines around her mouth and eyes, giving to her warm and inviting smile. Her beautiful blue eyes instantly give away her relation to Logan.

"Well, you must be Katelyn." Her voice is melodic and kind and when she wraps her arms around me, I take in the scent of what I am sure is my favorite Burberry perfume. "I am Sabina Blackwell, Logan's mother. It is such a pleasure to finally meet you."

I hesitate slightly but return the hug, hoping she cannot feel my heart beating hard against my chest.

She releases me and takes my hands in hers.

I smile at her and release a breath I didn't realize I was holding. "Thank you so much Mrs. Blackwell, though, the pleasure is mine. And thank you for having me in your beautiful home."

She waves her hand at me, "I will have none of that Mrs. Blackwell nonsense." She lets out a soft laugh, "Please, call me Sabina." She moves to stand between Logan and I and loops her arms through ours. "Now, come." She nudges us forward. "I will ask Harrison to bring us drinks and pastries on the patio."

I look at Logan and he shrugs his shoulders and mouths 'sorry.'

I giggle and mouth, 'It's ok.'

After stopping so that Sabina can speak briefly with Harrison, we walk with his mom out one of the three French double doors onto a beautiful patio with ceramic tile and two sets of wicker furniture. Down a small flight of steps is a walkway to a beautiful pool complete with rocks that double as slides and a waterfall. In the distance I see that a path leading down the back of the small hill to the dock where a rather large boat sits patiently.

She walks us over and leaves Logan and I to sit on a loveseat while she sits in a large single person chair. As soon as we make ourselves comfortable, Harrison steps out of a side door with a tray of pastries, chocolate covered strawberries, water with lemon for Logan and myself, and a cocktail for Sabina.

"I have to admit, Katelyn, I was unsure of whether or not Logan would bring you by to meet me." She raises her eyebrow at Logan with a smile.

Logan shakes his head. "Mother," he starts with a warning tone in his voice.

"See, our Logan has always been very private and has never given any indication regarding feelings for anyone, let alone allowing himself to be distracted. So, naturally I was quite intrigued when I heard him mentioning your name and smiling when he was texting on his phone-"

"Mother, are you serious? Did you want to meet her strictly to embarrass me?" Logan interrupts and sits back on the loveseat as he slides his hand beneath mine, interlocking our fingers.

"Oh, Logan," she huffs. "I hope I am not being too forward dear." She shifts her gaze to me and smiles.

"Oh, no. Not at all," I say, amused with the entire conversation.

"So, tell me about yourself, since I have not been able to get anything out of Logan beside your name."

A knot forms in my stomach and my body threatens to return the lunch we had earlier. Logan gives my hand a reassuring squeeze, but it only slightly helps.

"Oh, um... there isn't much to tell, really. I just graduated today, I work with my dad and stepmom at the ice rink they own over in Cove."

"She graduated with top honors and at the top of her class." Logan added, smiling proudly.

"Well, it doesn't surprise me that the one who has managed to attract my boy is smart *and* beautiful." She leans forward, grabbing a small rounded pastry puff and eases it into her mouth.

"Thank you," I say lowly, my gaze dropping quickly to

the floor where I am shifting my feet.

"Hhmmm, and humble as well." She looks at Logan. "I like her." She brings her gaze back to me. "Katelyn, Logan's father will be in town next weekend and I would love if you could join us for dinner."

"Um, sure, I just have to make sure that my dad and Liz don't need me at the rink. Thank you so much for inviting me." The knot in my stomach feels heavier.

All of a sudden, the double doors beside me fling open and a tall suited man steps out. Erebos. Immediately his gaze is drawn to me. I steal a glance at Logan who by now has sat up taller, moved closer, and moved my hand into his lap. Sabina raises an eyebrow at Erebos in a clear warning.

I don't know if Logan can see hear it or see it, but my breathing is suddenly trying to move at warp speed.

"My apologies, Sabina and Logan, I was unaware that you were to have company this afternoon."

"Funny, Erebos, I distinctly recall you lurking in the doorway when I was telling my mother that I would like to bring Katelyn by today."

"It must have slipped my mind, how rude of me," his words slide off his tongue like a snake.

Despite Logan's rigid posture and cold demeanor towards him, Erebos does not excuse himself. In fact, he steps closer and extends his hand. "We have not been properly introduced. I am Erebos."

I reluctantly extend my hand, careful to control my emotions as I can see waves forming in the pool below. "I am Katelyn." I clench my teeth and call on the protective girl I have been for so many years. "Are you sure we haven't met?" I ask, trying to keep the sarcasm in my tone to a minimum.

I hear Logan let out a snicker behind me as he wraps his arm around my waist. I release Erebos's hand and take hold of Logan's arms around me, allowing a calm to help bring my breathing to a semi-normal rate.

Erebos's expression falls and I see him move his jaw a couple of times, as he squints his eyes. My head begins to pound, but I do not let on. "No. It was only in passing outside the sandwich shop."

"Erebos," Logan calls to him sternly, breaking the gaze he had locked on me. Logan nudges me to turn as he does the same. "Mother, we should be going."

Sabina gives a hard look to Erebos, clearly bothered with his interruption. "Alright, my dear." Logan stands and steps forward planting a kiss on his mother's head. Sabina moves past him and takes me into another embrace.

This may take some getting used to.

"It truly was a pleasure meeting you and I hope you will be coming by again." I could hear a bit of longing and disappointment in her voice.

"I will Mrs. Bl-... Sabina." I give her an extra squeeze before letting go.

Logan pulls me along behind him as we walk past her chair and exit through one of the other double doors without so much as a word to Erebos.

As soon as we enter the house, Logan turns and takes my face in his hands. "I cannot explain to you how awesome that was. You didn't let him intimidate you at all."

I feel my eyes get heavy and the pounding in my head moves to my ears. I glance out the windows of the doors and Erebos is staring straight at me.

Logan sees this and stands between myself and the windows, pulling me close to him. "Are you sure there is nothing you want to tell me now?"

"My head hurts so badly," I breathe onto his chest.

I try to control my emotions regarding the pain and nothing works. Then as if by magic, I hear Mr. Wentworth's voice in my head. It wasn't only the elements, but the energies around them. So I think of the calm that being with Logan usually brings me, and though I feel the calm, I cannot shake the pain.

"Maybe you should lie down," Logan whispers onto my head.

"No, I probably just need an aspirin or something." I pull my head back and look into his eyes. "I don't want to ruin the plans you have for today."

"You won't ruin them. Come on." Logan nudges me forward and we walk toward the stairs. I barely remember the steps it took for us to get to the top. Once there, Logan leads us down a hallway to the left until it dead ends at a door. He turns the handle and when we walk in, I see a seating area with two loveseats, a leather recliner, and a fire place. He leads me in, closing the door behind us.

"You can lie down on my bed." Logan stretches out his arm to the wall with the door to our right.

You've got to be kidding. He basically has his own living room!

I shake my head "No, it's starting to subside. I'll be fine."

Logan smiles. "I know exactly what might help." He walks to a set of french double doors next to the entrance to the bed area and we step onto a balcony that wraps around the corner. There is iron furniture with burgundy cushions that he leads me to, but instead I grab hold of the rail and take in the beautiful ocean view. Below us you can see a glorious flower garden with a small fountain in the middle. Behind it, a set of trees leads directly to a drop off to the ocean. The view is breathtaking and I allow the scents of the flowers and the ocean to overcome me. Logan stands beside me and wraps his arm around me. I lean in closer, placing my head onto his chest and breathe deep, the pain slowly releasing its grip on my mind.

"Better?"

I nod.

"I'm sorry, Angel," he sighs and brings one of his hands to caress my cheek while the other stays wrapped around my back. "I had no idea my mom would invite you to meet my dad, and even less that Erebos would be here. I thought he had more sense than that." He pulls me tight. "I didn't like the way he looked at you at all. It took everything I had to keep from punching him.

"It's ok. Like I said, I still can't prove that it was him I saw, so I can't say anything, but damned if I was going to let him intimidate me." I turn to face him. "I hope your mom doesn't think I'm too forward or something."

"No. My mom doesn't like Erebos too much either. She deals with him because he is my dad's uncle."

"Oh." I feel bad momentarily for possibly starting trouble between family again but it doesn't last long. Something is off with Erebos and if trouble will keep him away from them, then that would be a good thing.

Logan keeps his hand on my cheek and I press into his palm. "You have the strangest effect on me." He pinches his eyebrows at me and gives me a wicked smile, suddenly making me think I should have chosen other words. "Well, I guess I should say effects because first you make it very hard to keep my walls up since you just walk in and barrel them down. Secondly, every time I am around you and I'm upset, you just hold me and I start feeling calm."

"Well, that's a good thing, right, Angel?" He leans down and presses his forehead to mine, taking my locket in his hand and turning it over.

"Yes," I say, my voice just above a whisper, my gaze on his remarkably blue eyes.

"This looks beautiful on you." He runs his thumb over the front of the locket.

"My dad and Liz gave it to me this morning as a graduation present. It has his family crest and my birth mother's family crest inside. He figured pictures would be kind of cheesy and not my style." Logan steals a glance at me raising an eyebrow. "Oh, he was right of course."

He laughs out loud and I realize how much I like hearing it. "Are you feeling better?" he places a short and gentle kiss on my forehead.

"Always when I'm around you, Polo."

Logan laughs again and takes me by the hand. "Then I get to show you one last thing before we go." His lips curl in a mischievous smile as he pulls me inside, closing the door behind us. He walks me past the sofas and the fireplace and up to a bookshelf that covers the entire wall. The whole thing is made of sectioned smaller bookshelves, each about three and a half feet wide, reaching from the floor to the ceiling.

Beautiful carved molding surrounds each individual bookshelf, but is cut so that side-by-side they create a grander piece. Logan walks to the last shelf and I see several books with old covers, some worn, some looking rather new.

"Have you read most of these?"

I see him blush for likely the first time in front of me and I feel I have discovered a secret. "Yes, pretty much all of them. I have an e-reader, but it's just not the same to me as holding a book in my hand and having the feel of turning the pages."

Just then, my heart swells a little knowing that I had given a similar reason to my dad and Liz for not wanting an e-reader of my own. "I know exactly what you mean," I say, sounding a bit breathier than I would have liked.

He looks at me for a moment, then turns his attention back to the last shelf. Shakespeare's works, The Greatest Works of Edgar Allen Poe, Sherlock Holmes, and Dracula; this entire section was strictly classic works. He reaches for The Secret Garden by Francis Hodgson Burnett, pulling it out almost completely, then pushing it down and back into the shelf. Immediately I hear the sound of several locks coming undone. The shelf unhinges and swings forward just enough and the book pops back up into place. Logan reaches over and takes the now exposed door, pulling it open.

My mouth drops open and I just gape at the secret passage he's just revealed.

Logan laughs out loud and gently pushes my mouth closed. "Yeah, I kind of thought you would like this." He takes my hand and pulls me in. He reaches over and grabs a latch, pulling the door shut and plunging us into complete darkness. I hold tighter to his hand as I press my back against the wall for stability. "Just need to get my phone." I hear his clothes rustling and suddenly a light comes on, giving the eerie room a more romantic feel. I look at his lips and wish he'd kiss me, but he just looks at me and slightly shakes his head, letting out a sigh, "Come on."

About five more feet in front of us is a winding staircase that leads to another small closet-sized room with two doors. He reaches in and turns the latch on the door to the left and sunlight begins to pour onto us as we step outside.

He closes the door behind us and as it blends so seamlessly with the building you begin to wonder where you came out of. "Wow. That is just like from the pages of a book," I say as my eyes dart around us, finding the beautiful garden to our right.

"That's what I thought when I first discovered it. I was unpacking my books and rearranging some of them that were already there when I came upon it. I have a funny feeling there may be a latch around here somewhere to get in, but for now I haven't found one."

"Where does the other door lead?" I ask with a big smile

on my face and an itch to go back in and find out myself.

"Oh, that leads to the den," he says matter of factly.

Sure, the den, you know, the room that everyone has... pft. "So where to now, Mister Full of Surprises?"

Logan gives a cute crooked smile. "To your car."

"And then?" I ask excitedly, hoping he will finally give in and tell me.

He glances at his watch. "You will find out soon enough.

CHAPTER 8

When we arrived at my car, Logan asked if he could drive so he could still keep as much of his plans a surprise as he could. I relented and tossed him the keys to my new baby. As soon as we pulled out of his driveway he pulls out his phone and makes a call.

"Are we ready?" His tone is very business-like, and I can't say I mind hearing him talk like that.

I try to lean over, to see if I hear anything, but he switches to his left ear so that the phone is farther from me. I squint my eyes at him and pout a lip but he only shrugs his shoulders in return.

"Very well, we will be there shortly." He smirks and hangs up his phone. "Slick, but not slick enough." he chuckles.

"Hey, the worst effort is the one never made!" I say as he takes my hand and plants a kiss on it.

"I hope you like it."

"I like just being with you. Anything else is a plus." I astound myself with the sudden confession and wonder if I should have said that.

Within a few minutes, Logan is turning into the Shippan Yacht Club and I quickly assume that he made reservations at the restaurant at the top of the building, though I have heard that reservations for that restaurant need to be made weeks and sometimes months in advance.

"So, do you think you know yet?" he asks as he pushes the shift into park.

"Maybe." I squint my eyes at him and press my lips together.

"I doubt it," he says chuckling as he opens the door.

"Ugh! The suspense is killing me already," I blurt before he exits the car and as the valet opens my door, prompting a smirk from him.

"Trust me, you won't have to wait long." He puts his hand out and helps me down, ensuring that I'm not flashing the valet as I slide off the seat.

We walk in through the sliding glass doors and I see shops lining the hallways to the left and right with marble floors leading the way. We don't go into any of the hallways or stop at the elevators before walking out the exit leading to the marina.

"Good evening sir, my name is Ronald, is there anything I can help you with?" we are greeted by an enthusiastic and very well-mannered gentleman probably in his late twenties, dressed in white slacks and a navy polo shirt with the Yacht Club insignia on it. His high and tight haircut and precise movements make me wonder if he was in the military at one point.

"Yes, I am Logan Blackwell the third. I spoke to you earlier."

Ronald smiles as he looks at me and then back to Logan. "Indeed you did, sir, one moment." He walks over to a small desk and picks up a phone, punching in only a few numbers. He has a very short conversation and returns to us. "Follow me."

Ronald leads us down the main path until we reach a sign that reads Dock 3. He steps to the side and puts his hand out indicating for us to continue. We begin our walk and a swarm of butterflies make their way into my stomach. At the end of the dock stands a man at attention, his hands clasped behind him. He is also wearing white slacks, but his polo is black and has the name of the boat he is standing next to, Lady of the Sea, scrawled across the left breast.

The enormity of what Logan may have planned begins to sink in and I am overwhelmed. I stop before we reach the man who is waiting for us.

"What is it?" Logan stops and moves to stand in front of me. "Angel?"

"I can't," is all I could say.

"I asked your dad and Liz and they said that you don't get seasick."

I shake my head. "No, I mean, this is too much," I sigh. "I can't let you do this."

His furrowed brow releases and pain and disappointment take its place. "Seriously? Now? You're going to push me away now?" He takes my hands in his. "Angel, we have had an amazing week and I just wanted to do this as both a graduation and birthday present."

I cock my head to the side as I realize how much planning must have gone into it. "I don't mean that I don't appreciate it, it's just that ... well, I'm not used to..."

"I'm sorry if this is too much, too soon, I just wanted to do something I know has never been done for you before." He puts his palm on my cheek. "Let me do this for you. Please."

I bite the corner of my bottom lip and stare into his eyes. "Okay." The corners of his lips rise until the smile reaches his eyes.

He moves beside me again and we walk toward the red-headed man awaiting us.

"Good evening, Mr. Blackwell, Miss Miller. Welcome to the Lady of the Sea. I am Mr. Brody and I will be your captain this evening." His Irish accent is light, but still noticeable.

"Thank you, Mr. Brody." Logan begins.

"Right then, if you will follow me." Mr. Brody turns and begins walking up the gangplank. The yacht that we are boarding is easily eighty feet in length, if not more. As we walk up, there is a group of people wearing the same uniform as the captain waiting for us. They each greet us as cordially as the captain and advise us that they are there for anything we need.

"I only need to verify a few things Mr. Blackwell, and we can set sail."

"Thank you, Captain," Logan says over his shoulder.

He walks me to the front of the amazing vessel as we grab hold of the railing.

It's not long before we begin moving and soon we are on the open sea, with the wind making its way through my hair. The pain in my feet from wearing the heels all day begins to bother me, so I walk over to a bench that sits along the open railing and close my eyes, allowing the wind and the salty air to consume me. Logan comes and sits behind me putting his arms around me. I lean back onto him and tilt my head so that my lips are near his ear. "I'm sorry."

"For what?" he asks lowly but doesn't move to look at me.

"For seeming ungrateful earlier." I push up and snuggle closer to him. "No one has ever done anything for me so amazing except my dad and Liz, and certainly not something to this scale."

"I know, it's probably because you always push everyone away." He leans his head to the side so that my lips are now grazing his ear. "I guess in a way, it's not an entirely bad thing, because I may not be here if that were not the case."

"You have a point," I whisper into his ear and I can feel the goosebumps on his arms. "I still don't know how you did it. How you managed to knock down those walls."

"Well, I can be pretty stubborn," he chuckles. "Plus, I don't know. There is just something about you. That first day I met you something said if I didn't find you again, if I didn't push my way in, I would regret it."

I lift my head away from his and turn to face him, sliding my legs to sit right over his, Logan's strong arms still tight around me. After I adjust my legs and body I look up to find his face no more than an inch from mine. This time I bring my hand to his cheek, and he presses into my palm. I inch my face closer until our noses touch. I can see the shimmering light blue in his eyes and the dark blue rim surrounding it.

He lifts his hand to my jaw, caressing my cheek with his thumb, bringing his lips to lightly brush against mine. I lean in, wanting more, and he presses his soft lips to mine. My hand makes its way to the back of his head and my fingers entangle themselves in his locks. The wind blows my hair all around us, and it seems as if there is nothing in this world at the moment but us, but this amazing feeling of his lips on mine.

He pulls back for a moment, but our noses are still touching. "You have no idea how long I have wanted to do that." He kisses me again, this time, stronger, and with more passion.

Now I pull back, grazing his lips once with mine. "Why didn't you?" I skim his lips again with mine, feening him.

"I wanted it to be perfect for you," he whispers onto my lips.

I pull tight on him and press my lips against his, opening just slightly to let him in. Every nerve in my body cries to be closer to him, to pull him nearer to me.

He entangles his fingers in my hair while his soft lips continue to caress mine.

The winds whip around us hard. I focus on only my feelings for him and accepting my emotions. Within seconds the winds begin to slow down.

We stop, but neither of us is willing to move and release ourselves from the closeness we have achieved.

"I was starting to worry that I was going too fast for you," Logan whispers onto my mouth.

"I thought that we were moving fast, too, but nothing about this feels wrong. I've never had such a desire to be near someone the way I do when I'm with you." I brush my lips to his quickly but softly. "I never thought I would say this to anyone, but I'm glad you didn't let me push you away. I'm glad you broke down those walls."

Logan kisses my nose and I drop my head to his neck, snuggling with him, loving that there is nothing around to bother us or take us out of this moment. We sit that way for another ten minutes until one of the staff comes to tell us that dinner is ready.

We follow the hostess across the deck and down a couple of steps into a cabin where there is a round table with a white tablecloth laid out over it, white plates with silver detailing, and silverware sitting next to it. On one of the plates sits a long silver box with a black bow around it.

An older gentleman walks over and pulls out the seat for me to sit in front of the box.

"More?" I pinch my brow.

"Last one for tonight, I promise."

I smirk at him and shake my head.

"Well, open it," He says as he leans forward on the table and smiles wide.

I take the silver box and unravel the bow, letting it fall to the plate. I pull open the box as far as its little hinges will allow, exposing a black velvet cushion holding a platinum bracelet. In the very center of the bracelet is a ruby, my birthstone, with an angel wing linked to the left and one linked to the right. The ends of the angel wings connect to a beautiful chainmail bracelet that alternates between large and small rosettes which lead to the clasp.

"Logan," I whisper as I run my finger over the beautiful and certainly custom made bracelet.

He stands from his seat and moves to be next to me. "Do you like it?"

I look up at him with my eyes filled with tears I am trying not to allow to fall. "I love it." I say, standing up and taking his face in my hands as I place my lips on his.

"May I?" he asks as soon as we stop.

I shake my head and he reaches for the silver box, taking the delicate bracelet out. He brings it up and over so that it is sitting perfectly on top of my wrist with the ruby in the center and the angel wings curving around. It is a stunning bracelet. "My Angel," he says as he clasps it shut and gives me a soft kiss before returning to his seat.

"Wow, today has truly been an unreal day."

Logan cocks his head slightly and smiles.

"First, the locket." I reach up to my necklace and open it, showing him the crests inside. "Then, the car. Finally, graduating that wretched school, as well as hearing you call me your girlfriend, meeting your mom, you renting a yacht for the evening, and a custom bracelet."

Logan laughs loudly. Not just a casual laugh, but from his gut laugh.

"What?" I ask as I run my finger along the bracelet, not sure what was so funny.

"You listed all these big gifts and nerve wracking events, and in there was me calling you my girlfriend?"

I feel the blush hit instantly. "Well, yes, I mean... with us moving so fast, and not knowing if we should be, I wasn't sure if I should consider myself that or not, let alone be the first to say it, or-" I drop off as Logan reaches across the table and grabs my hands.

"You are adorable when you ramble."

There's that damn blush again.

"And when you blush."

I knew it!

I drop my gaze to my plate for a moment and then back to him. "Thank you for not giving up on me so easily, for calling me out, for this week, for today..." I sigh and smile. "Just... thank you."

"Believe me when I say it is my pleasure." His blue eyes sparkle under the lights.

After a few moments of conversation regarding the immensity and beauty of the sailboat, the servers bring us our dinner of lobster and filet mignon. It isn't until we are having the delicious chocolate cake for dessert that Logan asks about my head.

"Oh," I say, swallowing the decadence in my mouth. "it's much better. It was almost gone when we were leaving your house."

"Wow, that's kinda strange. Do you get those often?" His brows come together slightly as he takes my hand.

"Recently." I put my fork down, unable to fit another bite.

"Like since your disappearance, recently?" His head tilts to the side.

"Yes." I answer at barely a whisper.

"Like whenever Erebos is around," he says plainly, finally saying what I think he wanted to say.

I bite my lip. "Maybe."

Logan releases my hand and leans back in his chair, one arm laying across his chest while his other hand reaches up, rubbing his chin. His gaze fixed on me.

"What?" I ask cautiously.

"I'm wondering if you will tell me what it is you couldn't tell me Tuesday at your house."

My heart drops into my stomach and I worry that dinner may reappear. "I… I can't."

His gaze softens and I can see the disappointment in his eyes. It's like he doesn't have to say anything to call me out.

"I... I need some air." I put my hand over my stomach trying to calm it as I put the napkin on the plate, push back my chair and walk out of the cabin. As soon as I walk out the air hits my face and I know by the feel of it, my skin is clammy. I look down at my hands and they're shaking. The water around us begins to roil and the waves pound the ship. I feel something welling inside of me and I can't figure out if it's anger, hurt, frustration, or something else entirely.

I make my way to the back of the boat and steady myself on the railing as I watch clouds gather in the distance. The conversation of Erebos and my secret have turned my insides and I cannot seem to calm them.

"Angel?" I hear Logan approaching and despite my attempts to calm myself, I only feel more anxiety.

Tears start streaming down my face and years of 'incidents' and secret keeping flash before my eyes. Images of Sam and her friends lying on the ground because of me, because of something I did paint my eyelids so I cannot even close my eyes for comfort.

"Stop," I say, though only to myself, begging these emotions to cease their assault on me.

"Katelyn." I feel Logan standing behind me.

I am holding onto the railing so tight my knuckles are turning white. The yacht begins to rock as some of the staff come out to tell us that we should hold on while the captain gets us to calmer waters. I feel the boat begin to move beneath us and watch the water we leave behind turning over on itself.

Logan wraps one arm around my waist and the other around my chest and arms as he puts his lips next to my ear. "Talk to me, baby. Tell me what's wrong."

My mind tries to register the fact that he may already know. "I can't." I cry, more tears streaming down my face. My legs become weak, but I manage to keep upright.

"Then just focus on me. Remember what you said you feel when I hold you? The calm?"

I turn in his arms and just before I bring my head down to rest on his chest, I see my reflection in his eyes. My iris glow the bright blue that Mr. Wentworth said the other kids described and I wonder if Logan saw.

I begin to feel the calm emanating from his touch and all the emotions, memories and apprehensions stop fighting for attention in my mind and body and settle into coherent thoughts. I wonder for a moment if it is something in him, or if this is something I take from him, because my powers allow it. The thought frightens me, but not enough to let go of him.

"Are you ok?" I ask Logan as I pull my head off his chest, leaving his dress shirt covered in my tears. "Oh, gosh, I am so sorry." I put my hand on his shirt.

"It's fine, I'm fine. I should be asking you if *you* are ok!"

I search his face for any sign of exhaustion to see if I pulled from his energy to feel the calm, but he looks fine. For a moment I think of a character from a comic book who takes other's energy and remind myself that something like that couldn't be possible. Or could it? A sudden urge to speak to Mr. Wentworth eats at me.

I glance behind us and the storm clouds that had begun to gather begin to slip away.

The captain rushes out onto the deck, "My apologies, Mr. Blackwell and Miss Miller, there was no storm on the weather report for tonight, I have no idea where that came from. I hope you two are alright."

"We're fine, Mr. Brody," Logan responds for us.

Mr. Brody takes a look at me and squints.

I realize that my tearstained face contradicts what Logan responded, so I add, "It's just been an emotional day... Graduation, my birthday, meeting parents." I give a clenched teeth smile, and strain my neck a bit, hoping he sees the humor and judging by his chuckle, he does.

The captain gives a smile. "I understand completely, Miss Miller." He turns on his heel and walks away.

"Was it that bad meeting my mother?" Logan chuckles.

"No, but it sounded better than saying, 'oh, nothing just having a meltdown because crazy stuff happens around me that I can't explain, and there is this guy that totally gives me the creeps, that I encountered today and I'm pretty sure my boyfriend is two seconds from thinking I am completely crazy and committing me to an asylum.'"

Logan laughs so hard he is on the verge of tears, causing me to laugh as well. I revel in the sound of his laugh and the calm that surrounds us now. He walks me over to a wicker sofa where we sit and look up at the crescent moon and the bright stars. He puts his arm around me and I lean on him, putting my hand on his leg, caressing his knee.

"Oh, and for the record, I don't think you are crazy. I would like to know what it is you can't tell me yet, but I suppose I can wait until you are ready. And to be honest, Erebos gives lots of people the creeps, and probably migraine headaches." He kisses the top of my head.

I laugh at the truth of the last part of that sentence and then question why. Does Erebos really have the power to try and get into my head and if so, why me?

CHAPTER 9

I wake up on my birthday to a room full of balloons, chocolate and a gift card to the bookstore from Dad and Liz. I convince Liz that the bags under my eyes are because I had just had such a great day yesterday that I couldn't sleep last night. The last thing I want to tell her is that every hour or so, I was up with nightmares about not being able to control my powers, Erebos chasing me, and Logan leaving me. Part of me is exhausted and part of me wants to get the day going so that I can find and speak to Mr. Wentworth.

I realize that he may or may not be in school today since some teachers are still there the week after school is out, getting paperwork done. But, considering he isn't a teacher that would just be luck of the draw. I remember him saying that his powers include a psychic connection of sorts and considering that he is always looking after me, I decide to go to the last place we met in the hopes that he will show up.

I look at my phone. Ten eighteen in the morning and I already have seven texts to sort through. I have one each from Ana, Dad, Liz, and my grandparents in California. The rest are from Logan, asking how I am feeling today, wishing me a happy birthday and asking if I have plans because he wants to spend time with his girl.

I reach over to my nightstand where my dad placed a birthday card to me from him and Liz, and one from my mother's aunt. Every year she sends me a card and every year I wonder about her briefly before going about my day, I always figured that the less people I had in my life the better.

For the first few years, I would talk to her on the phone and we even visited with her a couple of times, but after Samantha's party, I pushed everyone away that I could. I pick up her card and turn it over in my hands. Evangeline Adams, Salem, Mass. *Geez, the irony in that is ridiculous.* I open the card slowly, as if the card was about to reveal some secret about my mother or her family that I needed to know.

Dear Katelyn,

Happy Birthday, beautiful girl. I know it has been a while since I have seen you, but your father has been gracious enough to always send me pictures of you and let me know how you are doing. Congratulations on graduating at the top of your class. Your mother would have been so proud. I can only imagine how exciting it must be for you to turn eighteen. I remember your mother turning eighteen as if it were only yesterday. It was quite a memorable year.

I understand if you still want to keep your distance, but please remember that I am always here for you if you ever want to visit, come by and talk, have questions about your mother, or anything else.

I hope this card finds you well.

Love Always,
Your Great-Aunt Eva

I look at the card, noticing that she has underlined certain words. *Well, it may not have revealed a secret, but damned if she doesn't know something.* I consider calling her, but then decide that maybe I should pay her a visit. I text my dad to ask if I can make a drive to Boston to check out the campus tomorrow. I decide to leave out the part where I will be driving the extra hour to visit my great aunt for now.

I fold the card and put it in my messenger bag then head to the shower to begin my day and hopefully get some answers.

I pull up to the beach and park just behind the bench where I last sat with Mr. Wentworth. There is a lady sitting there watching her son play with a remote control car, so I wait for her to decide to leave. She lasts about ten minutes before packing up their things and walking away. I step out of my Jeep slowly and walk over to sit on the bench, my gaze on the ocean in front of me. I stare at some of the small waves in the water, forcing some to become just slightly bigger than the others. *Well, at least I can control some of it.*

"I was wondering how long it would take," Mr. Wentworth's voice comes from behind me, but I do not move to meet his gaze. Instead, I look down at my fidgeting hands.

He walks around the bench and sits beside me. He's dressed the most casual that I have ever seen him. His blue jeans are a bit worn on the knee and his sneakers are meticulously kept. His black shirt matches the black Nike ball cap he has on.

"I wasn't sure if you'd be here. I didn't know how this worked," I say, sneaking a glance out of the corner of my eye. He looks much more handsome when he isn't in work clothes and glaring at me with his 'I know something you don't know stare'. Very much like a TV dad or something.

He chuckles and leans forward onto his elbows. "It's kind of hard to explain. I don't know what you are thinking, unless I am directly in front of you and you are unguarded, but if you need to find me and think about it enough, I just know." His lip pulls into a half smirk. "Happy birthday, by the way."

"Oh. Thank you." I smile, not aware that he knew.

"So, what did you want to talk about?"

"I have tons of questions, but I guess I'll start with the ones that bug me the most." I tilt my head so I am looking at him.

He returns the look, "Shoot."

"You said that there are others, correct? Do all of us have the same abilities?"

"I did say that there are others, but no, you do not all have the same abilities, nor has there ever been a family with powers as strong as the Langleys and Blackbournes since they came into existence. Powers can evolve and can also be watered down by different bloodlines. Some remain with the elements, some transfer to healing, psychic ability, and some so minimal, people may not even know they possess them."

"Have you heard of ones who can try to read minds, or get inside them, or something like that?"

"Yes. They are powerful. It may not necessarily mean that they are of the Blackbourne lineage or the Langley lineage, but it shouldn't be discounted." He sits up, leaning his arm on the back of the bench. "Why?"

"The guy who was in the forest that day that you saved me, I saw him for the second time and my head pounded like crazy when he was looking at me."

"Hm, I have been trying to find him, but I didn't get a good look at his face. Do you know his name? I can try to find out more about him."

"His name is Erebos. His last name might be Blackwell, but I am not sure."

Mr. Wentworth moves his jaw a couple times and squints his eyes as if making some mental notes.

"You… you said you knew my mother. Did you know her aunt as well? Did she or my mom have powers?"

"Evangeline." He smiles fondly and I wonder just how well he knows her. "She does have powers as did your mother. Though because she raised your mother, she would best be able to tell you what your mother was capable of. She has waited for you to turn eighteen."

"Why? What happens at eighteen?" My heart begins to beat faster.

"All your powers develop and are more controllable and more powerful. You should be able to do more at your own will now, as opposed to things just happening. Remember though, as with anything else, you will require practice. Magic is not as easy to control as you might think."

"Trust me, I don't think that at all." I take off my sunglasses and rub some exhaustion from my face. "So what do I do if I see this, Erebos again?"

"Do what you have done every day of your life. Guard your emotions and your thoughts. That is the reason your head hurts so badly. You are so used to being guarded, you do it automatically and fight him off without trying. If he was able to get in your mind, you would feel a confusion of sorts or perhaps have difficulty concentrating." He folds his arms across his chest. "Regardless, I will find out what I can regarding him. Is there anything else you would like me to answer for you?"

"Well, there is one thing that has kind of eaten at me since it happened. How did you make me go from your house to the forest behind my house?"

Mr. Wentworth chuckles loudly and stands. "Would you rather I show you?" He extends his hand forward so that I would walk with him.

I stand wearily and walk with him to a small nearby forest. My heart begins to race and I start to wonder what is going to happen. I mean, yeah, he's been pretty helpful and all lately but, I still don't really know him and walking into a forest with a guy who can control magic may not be my best idea.

He begins looking around and stops when he finds two

trees that are parallel to each other. "Are you sure you want to know?"

I squint my eyes and pinch my eyebrows together as I nod.

Mr. Wentworth says some words in a language I have never heard and waves his hand in a circular motion between the two trees. As soon as he is done, he extends his hand to me. "Do not be afraid."

I place my shaking hand in his and as we both step into the space between the two trees our legs disappear from our sights. I look at him in horror, but he simply pulls my hand and continues forward. When we emerge we are standing in a forest I have never seen before. Huge willow trees and Junipers tower over us, and most of the daylight is gone. The skies are mostly grey and the smell of rain is potent. I slowly release his hand. "Mr. Wentw-,"

"Please, Gamaliel," He interrupts softly.

I look back between the trees we just came through and they are gone. All I see is this immense forest around us. I drop my gaze to him and realize that my mouth is gaping.

"Portals," he chuckles. "It is a very old magic and very few people can do it. In fact, probably the only ones left who can, are the Keepers of Balance, Angels, and Fallen Angels or Demons. But that's a whole other story."

"So, where are we?" I ask as I begin to walk forward with

a purpose I know I have but cannot define. "It feels so familiar." I call over my shoulder to him.

Gamaliel tilts his head, watching me and my heart falls into my stomach. Something is not right about this place. I continue through the trees turning at different intervals and even picking up the pace a couple of times. My sneakers pound against the soft earth and I feel the energies around me. I don't ask him again because I don't have to, I know I will find out eventually. I continue at such a pace that the trees around me seem like a blur, until I reach a clearing and I stop cold. I stand in the middle of it looking at Gamaliel who is standing along the edge.

The willow trees that surround me have a sadness that the others did not. I feel the pull again, but it's not to move in any direction, it is below me. I slowly drop to my knees and put my hands on the ground, twigs and dried leaves cracking beneath the pressure. The smell of the grass and the imminent rain assault my senses. I close my eyes and that is when I see it. Flashes of the Penhale massacres.

I see men and women being slain in their sleep, babies being ripped from their cribs or their weeping mother's arms. My tears hit the ground below me and the flashes come harder. Husbands defending their wives and children slain in front of them, their bodies dragged to a cart at the edge of town with horses at the ready. The larger homes, barricaded from the outside and set ablaze, burning the residents alive. I feel my arms start to shake, but I can't stop the onslaught. I see mothers racing through the fields with young ones in their arms only to meet the end of a sickle as it is brought down upon them with a terrible force. There are few who make it to the safety of the forest but I cannot see if they live. The rain begins to fall hard and the blood of the fallen drips from the cart, staining the streets with the blood of the Langleys.

My eyes spring open and I release a scream from the depths of my soul. I feel the pain radiate through my body and a flash of bright blue light erupts from my hands out into the forest around us. Gamaliel walks to me slowly as I sit back on my heels, staring at my hands, then raise my gaze to him. He regards me with a sadness, as if he can feel my pain. Then I think that perhaps he can. Perhaps, he was there. "This is where they buried them, isn't it?"

"Yes."

I shake my head and tears fall from my eyes. "Do any of them still live? From that time? Are any like you, immortal?"

"No." He kneels in front of me and takes my hands, wiping off the dirt and leaves. "But there are still a few who believe the way they did then, that have killed members of your family in search of the one."

"In search of me?" I wipe my face with the back of my hand.

"Katelyn, I have to tell you something. In all the years I have watched over your family, none have been able to find the resting place of your ancestors. Some tried, but failed, others did not try at all. But you, it called to you, it pulled you to it. You... you are the White Witch, the hope who will stop the Blackbournes who continue to hunt your family." Gamaliel helps me up and leads me to another set of parallel trees where he makes a portal to go home.

I take one more look around me, taking in the sights and smell, and just as the rain begins to fall, we walk through.

"I had no intention of ruining your birthday," he says as he presses his lips together.

I take a deep breath, trying to calm my spirit and I feel a need to be near Logan. "You didn't ruin it. Thank you for taking me there. What now, though?"

Gamaliel presses his lips together and sighs. "With you being eighteen and your powers being so strong, it is only a matter of time before they find you. You must practice and be prepared. I have to warn you, though, your family and your new boyfriend can be in danger. They may use anyone close to you to get to you. Do you understand?"

I shake my head and swallow the lump in my throat. "How do I find you if I need you?"

"You can do what you did today." He reaches into his pocket and pulls out a phone. "Or you can text me." He types out his phone number in a message and gives me the phone so that I can type in my own number. I shake my head and smile as I tap the screen saving my information. "What? Sometimes technology can be a bit more convenient than magic," he chuckles as I give him his phone. "I will see you soon."

"Katelyn!"

I hear my name being called and I turn in the direction where my car is. "I have to g-" when I turn again, Gamaliel is gone. I take a deep breath and begin walking toward the bench when I see Logan's car parked beside mine. I begin looking around and see Logan standing near a food stand in the distance.

I walk up the path feeling the sand scrape against the concrete walkway and I quickly look down at my hands and knees to see if there is any dirt on them from the forest. Nothing. It is as if I was never there.

"Angel!" Logan walks toward me in his black cargo shorts, black Nike sneakers, and grey shirt stretched across his pecks as his biceps force their way out of the sleeves. *Seriously? It's like he was plucked out of a magazine or something.*

"Hey!" I walk faster until I reach him and he wraps his arms around my waist, pulling me up off the ground and kissing my lips.

"Where've you been?" He kisses me again before putting me down. "I was driving by and saw your Jeep, so I pulled in.

I walked around everywhere and couldn't find you. I even texted you."

I pull my phone out of my pocket and check the screen, but I have no missed calls or messages. I turn the phone to face him, so he could see.

"Wow, that is weird." He pulls out his phone verifying that he sent them. "I'll have to call the cell company and see what's up with my phone."

I wonder briefly if it had to do with me walking through a portal and being on the other side of the world. *Um maybe*, I giggle to myself.

"Anyway, happy birthday, baby." He leans down giving me another kiss. "Just came down for a walk on the beach?"

"Yeah, I also like to walk the trails sometimes to clear my head."

"Oh." Logan takes a step back. "Do you want me to go? I don't want to barge in on your chill time or anything. I know you probably feel like I'm freakin' suffocating you by now."

I furrow my brow and slap him playfully on the arm. "I think no such thing! I love hanging out with you, and no, I do not want you to leave. As a matter of fact, I was actually just thinking of you when I heard you call out my name."

"Really?" Logan steps forward, wrapping his arm around me. "What were you thinking of?"

"This." I lift up on the balls of my feet and press my lips

to his.

"Mmm, I like thinking of this." He smiles on my lips as he takes a step back. "I gotta say, someone is looking pretty damn sexy today."

I look down at my black fitted tank top, my jeans and my sneakers. "Um, sexy was yesterday. This is regular old me."

Logan grabs my hand and pulls me close. "Yesterday was stunning and yes, sexy. But there is nothing sexier than when you are being you."

I smile and reach down into my pocket where Paul Simon's Father and Daughter is playing and a picture of my dad is flashing on my screen. "Hey, dad." I listen as my father begins to tell me that he'd rather I leave the Boston trip for a weekend that he and Liz can come with me. "I know, dad, but I was thinking that this way, I can see what it's like to make the drive because there will be times if I go there, that I will be coming down to see you. It will only be a day trip. I should be back by nightfall. I promise." I roll my eyes and Logan huffs a laugh. "Yes, we will make the trip together in a couple of weekends… Okay… Love you too."

"Paul Simon?" Logan questions.

"Hey, I may be a sarcastic badass, but deep down I'm still daddy's girl."

He lifts his hands, freeing himself of accusations. "Hey, I thought it was pretty cute."

I squint my eyes at him.

"So, not that I was eavesdropping, but what drive are you making?"

"Oh!" I start, completely not thinking of what Logan would say or if he would ask to come. "I just wanted to take a drive out to Boston tomorrow and take a walk around the campus."

"Oh, okay. You alright going alone? I can go with you if you want." The corner of his lip rises.

"I think it would be good for me to go by myself. Just to get an idea of what the drive will be like and all that, since I'm leaning toward going to that school anyway."

Logan looks me over. "Okay. That's a good thing anyway, because then you won't be too far from me." His smile grows wider. "So, birthday girl, what are your plans for today?"

"I didn't really have any. I was thinking of swinging by the rink to see how things are going and I definitely wanted to see you. So I guess that works out pretty well, seeing as how you are already here, maybe you can come with?" I bat my eyelashes at him and smile.

Logan laughs. "Which car?"

"Hm," I look at my new Jeep and then back to him. "Why don't we drop the Jeep off at my house and then go to the rink?"

I pull into my driveway and as I lock my car and walk to

Logan's Tahoe that is running idly in the street, I see a silver gun metal grey SUV stopped down the street. I had never seen that vehicle before, and though I can't make out the person sitting inside because of the dark tinted windows, I do know that someone is sitting there. I write myself off as paranoid and get into Logan's SUV.

"You okay?" Logan asks before shifting into drive and pulling away from the curb.

"Yep." I smile and it seems to satisfy him.

The drive to the rink is quiet for the most part. I find myself looking in the sideview mirror a few times and I think I see the SUV a couple of times, but I lose it quickly in the traffic. I see Logan checking his rearview a few times as well, and I wonder if he is trying to see what I am looking at. He reaches over and slides his hand over mine, entwining our fingers together. I find myself drifting to this morning's events and Gamaliel's warnings. My heart becomes heavy with worry for Logan and my parents.

"Kate?" Logan squeezes my hand.

"Huh?" I shake my head from the daze.

"Hi, welcome back," he laughs at his reference of me spacing out. "We're here."

We step down from the SUV and I find myself searching the parking lot for the gunmetal grey SUV but I don't see it and am momentarily relieved.

We walk in to a bombardment of ice skaters, coaches, parents, siblings, and vendors.

"Wow!" Logan looks around at the enormity of the event and his gaze rests on the skaters warming up on the ice. "Holy crap! Did you see that? If I tried that I'd break my leg in like three places!"

I laugh out loud and pull Logan along through the crowd towards the back of the building where my father's office is.

I wave at a few of the employees and stop for some hugs and "Happy Birthdays" along the way.

"Wow, for someone who likes to push people away, you seem pretty popular here."

"Well, when you're the boss' daughter, it doesn't matter how weird you are, people will be nice to you."

Logan rolls his eyes. "I'm pretty sure it has nothing to do with you being the boss's daughter." I open the door to my dad's office and find him sitting at his desk eating a hotdog with Liz sitting across from him doing the same.

"Sneaking in a late lunch?" I laugh as we walk in.

"You saw how crazy it is out there." Liz chimes in with a sigh.

"Mr. and Mrs. Miller, we can go get you something else for lunch or dinner if you'd like." Logan says as he steps forward, still holding my hand.

"Very kind of you, Logan, but we will be fine with this.

Today's events finish at seven, so we will leave the staff cleaning up and either head home or ask if you two wanted to meet for dinner?"

"You guys are exhausted and we have celebrated my birthday like three times over. You two go home and next weekend or during the week we can all go out to dinner." I let go of Logan's hand and walk over, giving my dad a hug.

"I'm pretty sure I have the most thoughtful daughter in the world here, Logan," he says as he releases me and pats my back.

"That you do, Mr. Miller."

"Bah, we're past that. Besides, any man who can make my daughter smile the way you do, well…" My dad waves his hand in the air. "It'll be Rick and Liz, if you please." he chuckled.

"Thank you, Mr. Mi-… Rick." Logan smiles and I think I see his cheeks get a little red.

"So, what are you two up to tonight?" Liz gulps down what I am sure is her usual of water with lemon.

"Meh, just hanging out and maybe grabbing a bite later." I shrug my shoulders and slide my hand back into Logan's. "I'll text you guys later and keep you posted on what time I should be home."

I convince Logan to go to the coffee shop that we had been at on our first night together. Though it is pretty full, the red sofa we had sat on is vacant, so Logan tells me to go save it while he orders our chai lattes. I make my way over and sit down, though I cannot shake the feeling of someone watching me. I look around the coffee shop and everyone around is engrossed in conversations or playing on their phones, tablets, or laptops. *You're getting paranoid, Kate. Stop it.* My attention is drawn to the parking lot where I see the gunmetal grey SUV. *Shit.* I try to look inside, but again, the tints are so dark, there is no deciphering its inhabitants. I shift my gaze to Logan who is walking toward me and I smile. By the time I look back, the SUV is pulling out of the parking lot.

"Alright, what gives babe?" Logan plops himself down right next to me and rests his elbows on his quads.

"What do you mean?" I feign innocence, but I realize that my smile may not have been as genuine as I would have liked it to be.

"You know exactly what I mean." He rubs his face and sighs hard. "It's hard enough knowing that there is something you need to tell me, but won't. But keeping things from me all day, and lying when I ask you about them, I mean, how am I supposed to feel about that?"

I sigh and bury my face in my hands, feeling a wavy curtain of hair encircle me.

"You tell me that you think I am in danger, or you are in danger, or I am in danger because of you and you don't tell me what it is?" he says in a harsh whisper.

Michelle comes over with a round black tray filled with coffee mugs of all different shapes and sizes. She reaches for the only two that are identical and puts them on the table in front of us and winks at me. I smile weakly and look at the steaming cups of tea that I have suddenly lost my appetite for.

Logan shifts in the seat, sitting with one leg hiked up so he can face me, waiting.

"You're right," I finally admit, turning to sit in the same fashion, facing him. "I just…. gosh, this is so effing hard!" I drop my gaze to my fingers that have not stopped moving. I rack my brain trying to figure out where to start. "Okay, as for today, I'm sorry." Logan reaches forward, grabbing my hands, forcing me to stop my fiddling, and I look up at him. "I learned something this morning. Something about my past that was… well, *is*, pretty scary. It is the reason you and likely Liz and my dad are in danger." I drop my gaze again, but bring it back up. "I even… I even wondered if it would be better for you if I wasn't around you."

Logan furrows his brow and looks at me as though I have slapped him in the face. "Rather than allow me to face this with you? To help you, if I could?"

"That's just it," I sigh, not knowing how much to divulge, especially here. "I don't know that you can help me."

"Of course, not! You won't even tell me what it is that is

going on!" Logan turns and rubs his face again, stopping for a moment while he stares at the table. "Do you realize, that even without trying, you are pushing me away."

My eyes water. "Log-"

"Please, Katelyn, don't." He takes a deep breath and lets it out slowly, avoiding looking at me. "You know what's the hardest part about all this?" he finally lifts his gaze at me and his blue eyes are sparkling beneath the lights. "I think I already know and it doesn't bother me. And to be honest, if the roles were reversed, and you asked me," he puts a hand on my arm and a wave of calm rushes through me. Not a little at a time like before, but a calm I can feel coursing through my body. "I would have told you."

My eyes open wide and tears fall as my heart shatters.

"Come on, I'll take you home," he stands from the loveseat and what's left of my heart sinks into my stomach.

I shake my head, not wanting to move. I want to beg him to stay, but what right do I have?

"Don't do this, Katelyn."

I wipe my eyes, stopping myself from crying like I have done so many times before. Though it never hurt this bad and it never was so hard to do. I stand, looking at the two steaming cups of chai that we never touched. The only two cups on that tray that were identical. A wave of nausea consumes me as I walk behind Logan out of the coffee shop.

"I'm sorry." I say as we reach his Tahoe.

Logan stops, his back to me. "No, I'm sorry." He turns to face me. "I didn't mean for this to happen, especially not today, not on your birthday… it's just that…" He shrugs his shoulders and shakes his head as he opens the door.

I stand frozen, my gaze on the ground below me as storm clouds roll in, viciously consuming the sky above us and opening up onto us. The rain falls hard, pelting my skin, but I don't move, I only look up and see him standing there. I start to walk down the pathway away from his truck.

I hear him calling for me, but I don't turn around, my senses numb. I fill the sky with thunder and lightning and continue walking. I turn the corner of the strip mall where the coffee shop is and run into the alley, finding shelter beneath a backdoor awning. I barely hear him yell for me through the rain and thunder but I stay here. My insides turn over as I think of the hurt on his face and his own revelation to me, my heart, nothing more than a stone in my stomach.

I make it rain for another ten minutes, but I don't leave the shelter of the awning for a good thirty. My phone flashes with several missed phone calls and messages, but I can't bring myself to check them. I thank God for the waterproof case that my dad bought me when I first got my phone and call a cab to come pick me up.

As soon as I walk through the door, I head up to my

shower. I strip out of my wet clothes and leave them in a pile on the floor. I let the hot water warm every inch of my body as hot tears make their way down my cheeks. Logan called me out again and was right, again. I would have been just as hurt if he had done it to me. I probably would not have even stood for it as long as he did. After I dry myself, I pull out my favorite jeans from the closet and my tight quarter-sleeve black shirt. *I need to skate tonight*.

I sit on the edge of my bed with my phone in my hand and start scrolling through Logan's messages. My heart breaks more when I hear that he didn't want to leave me in the rain, that he even got out of his truck and searched for me. He apologized for letting it all get to him. But I know that it wasn't fair for me to do that to him. By the time I get to the most recent message he is asking me to tell him where I am because he is worried and feels like a complete jerk.

I hit the reply button and let him know that I made it home safe, but that I wouldn't be here much longer. His response is immediate and he asks if he can call me. I tell him that I wouldn't be good conversation right now.

I sit, staring at the phone and the time, realizing that I needed to get out of home, because I didn't want to be home when Dad and Liz got here. I certainly didn't want any questions about where Logan was, or why I was already home without him.

I pull on my black rider boots with buckles on them, grab my hoodie, and walk out the door. I drive out to the beach for a little where I watch the waves and try my hand at controlling the winds around me. I am successful a handful of times, but it doesn't last long. I stand to return to my Jeep and search for the gunmetal grey SUV, but I don't see it, which is a relief and at the same time, unnerving. I pull out my phone and text my parents to check in on them. Both at home relaxing, the nerves are calmed just a little bit.

I sit in my Jeep and stare at the picture of Logan that I have set as his caller ID. I take a deep breath and send a message.

Can you skate?

CHAPTER 10

As always, his response of 'yes' is immediate. I smile and ask him to meet me at the rink at ten. I park my Jeep in front of the main entrance and open my trunk so that I can sit inside on the edge to enjoy the night air while I wait for Logan. The scent of rain is gone and the breeze carries with it, the scent of the swamp azaleas that are planted around the larger white oaks surrounding the building.

I sit rocking my legs back and forth watching every set of headlights that slow down near the entrance hoping it's Logan. My heart jumps when a large set of lights turn into the parking area. The black Tahoe makes its way to the front of the building and parks right behind me. As he pulls up, he turns off his lights, probably so he doesn't blind me.

Logan steps out of the truck and I see that he has also changed his clothes. He is in jeans and wearing a blue polo that brings out his eyes. He has a set of hockey skates dangling from his hand as he closes the door.

"Angel,-" I hold up my hand as I walk up to him.

"It's my turn to talk," I say softly, though I don't immediately say anything else. Unsure if he wants to hold my hand, I just ask him to follow me.

I walk up to the door and insert my key, unlocking both deadbolts before swinging it open and running to the alarm control panel nearby and punching in a code. Logan closes and locks the door behind him, giving me a soft smile.

I grin at him as the swarm of butterflies are back in full force. I turn on only the lights over the hockey rink and we walk in the darkness toward it. I flinch from the surprise when I feel Logan's hand slide into mine, but I entwine my fingers with his and allow a smile to make its way across my face again. We walk in silence until we reach the bleachers where we sit down and begin to put on our skates.

"So, hockey skates?" I close my eyes. *Really? So, hockey skates? That's my first line after making him come over here?!*

"Lived in New York, remember?" he shrugs his shoulders.

As soon as he is done, he stands and waits for me to finish. He puts his hand out to help me up and we unlatch the door to the rink. I breathe in the smell of the ice and let the cold make its way up my body. I take Logan's hand and we begin skating along the boards, the entire length of the rink. By the third lap I begin to lose myself in the breeze in my hair, the smell of the ice and having Logan there with me. Though I don't make it happen, I feel the shavings of the ice and the snow lifting behind me, following as the bliss overtakes me.

"Can you skate backwards?" It's the first time I had spoken since I asked about his skates.

He pinches his brows. "Yes." He quickly turns and continues skating, keeping my pace. His eyes open wider as he looks behind me and his lips curl up into a smile.

I check the reflection in some of the glass and barely see the whirlwind of snowfall behind me.

"Wanna see something funny?"

Logan smiles at me and nods.

I turn to face the snow and just like last time, it all collapses to the ground.

"Hm, guess it doesn't like to be watched. Maybe it's just shy."

I giggle out loud as we slow down and I lean against the boards along the benches. A moment of silence overtakes us, but it's not awkward or uncomfortable.

"I...I'm sorry, I didn't trust you before. I was just..." I start weakly.

"Afraid?" Logan jumps in.

"Yeah. I didn't want you to see me the way everyone else did. Like a freak." My gaze is on the ice as I lean on my arms so I can move my skates back and forth.

Logan grabs my chin gently with his thumb and forefinger and slowly lifts my gaze to him. "I could never see you the way they do. In fact, I thought that was pretty damn cool. I've never seen that."

"You know, I was pretty shocked when you showed me your power," I blurt out, almost unsure of what to say next.

Logan gives a crooked smile. "I was hoping that maybe you would pick up on it and that it would make you comfortable enough with yourself to realize that there isn't anything wrong with you."

"Guess, I should have picked it up, huh?" I folded my arms across my chest. "I mean hell, I was close enough when I was saying that you have a calming effect on me."

"Well, I probably shouldn't have assumed that you would catch on to it. I didn't know how much you knew about our 'world'." He ends on the last word with air quotes. "And, I guess I was just pretty excited to have found someone who has gifts as well."

I blush at his words and realize how sweet it is that we share this. "So um, tell me, what powers have you seen?" I ask cautiously, continuing this venture into a conversation I

---

seriously never thought I would have.

"Well, I've never told anyone about my gifts so I haven't really met too many others, at least not that they have told me, who also has gifts."

Gifts..., hm, I guess that's one way to look at this.

"I discovered my gifts when I was a kid. I had a dog that was hit by a car and we took him to the vet, but there was nothing they could do for him. He was a nervous wreck, I could feel it every time I touched him. It was strange, it was like I could feel his emotions just by touch. He was so scared and in so much pain, so I thought, maybe if I could just be calm for him, he would pick up on it. But my mom who was watching the whole thing, knew that it was more than him catching onto it. He didn't even whimper anymore once I cradled him in my arms. He still died of course, but it wasn't as bad as it could have been."

"Oh gosh." I move to stand in front of Logan. "That's a hard way to find that out."

"Yeah," he huffs, but still smiles.

"So, um, your mom... does she have powers too?"

"Well, hers are more earth oriented. I guess you can say that she's got a seriously green thumb."

I laugh out loud and Logan reaches for the belt loop on my jeans and pulls me forward. I push off the board and listen to the sound of my skates on the ice.

"You made it rain earlier, didn't you?" He presses his forehead to mine.

"Yes. I wanted to tell you it was me, but I could barely believe it myself. I only recently began to figure out how to control this." I take in a deep breath and fix my eyes on his, which at the moment are soft and endearing and begging me to come closer. "I was so upset for having done that to you, I almost felt like I could hide in that rain. I wanted it to swallow me whole."

Logan smiles and tucks a tendril of hair behind my ear. "Don't stress over that." He waits for me to nod in agreement. "I take it your dad doesn't have gifts?"

I huff a laugh. "Only the gift of loving a daughter who to everyone else is strange."

Logan leans in and kisses me and it's only then that I realized how much I would have missed his kisses. The smell of soap and a soft but very manly cologne surround me and I breathe him in. "So besides the emotion transfer, is there anything else you can do?"

"Apparently fall for a certain girl faster than I ever thought possible."

I feel a heat consume me and though I want to respond, I can't.

"Other than that, I have a bit of elemental control, but nothing I've tried to master. A bit of healing, as in I heal a bit faster than most people, but nothing can transfer."

"Erebos has powers doesn't he?" I hate myself for ruining the moment, but I know I have to ask.

Logan purses his lips. "Yes. I haven't really talked to him about them because something about him has always kept me at a distance. But I know he does." He chews on his lip for a moment. "Is this why you think that I or your family are in danger?"

I smile at him and put my hand on his cheek. "This is why I know you are all in danger." I skate back and take his hand, nudging him to skate along with me, hoping that it will make it that much easier to explain. We take turns skating backwards so that we are always facing each other, the first few times in silence as I try to figure out how to explain it all. I begin by telling the stories of the 'incidents' I have had and finish with the most recent at school and on the yacht. I explain to him about Gamaliel, and who he is and what he has explained to me. I leave out the part about the portal because I'm not sure how much I should give away regarding the Keeper.

We make our way to the door of the rink and begin to take off our skates.

"Why don't we go to the coffee shop and keep talking?" Logan looks at me, with his sweet smile, his blue eyes eager for my response.

I look at my watch. Twelve o'clock. "Sounds good."

We drive over and make our way to our favorite sofa which luckily was clearing out as soon as we began placing our order.

"Everything ok with the chai's earlier? I saw that you guys didn't even take a sip." Michelle pouts behind the counter.

"Sorry about that Michelle, we had an…" I look at Logan quickly.

"An emergency," he finishes.

"Oh, wow, I hope everything is alright." She tries to give Logan back his change but he refuses and she drops it in the tip jar.

"Better than ever," Logan responds as he takes my hand.

I scan the parking lot and see the gunmetal grey SUV drive by. I look back at Logan, "Earlier when we were together, there was a gunmetal grey SUV that followed us."

He nods his head in agreement. "I saw it too."

"It's here again. I just saw it cross the parking lot."

Logan whips his head around, searching, but neither of us spot it now. "Are you going to tell your parents?" Logan asks before he looks back at me.

My parents? I never thought about telling them the extent of the truth about me. They were so alright with loving me anyway, despite these strange things, that I never thought in the last week that I would have to possibly crush their view of me.

"I... I don't know. I haven't gotten that far yet. I don't want them to worry about me." I look at Michelle as she comes with the same mugs she did earlier and places them in front of us.

"For the lovebirds," she says sweetly and walks away.

"You are also afraid of what they will think of you."

I sigh, still staring at the mug, "Yes."

"They will not think any differently of you. I promise." He takes my hand and we both lean back, Logan on the sofa and me on him. "And if you want me there when you tell them, so that they can see that you are not the only one, then I will show them who I am, too."

I lift my head quickly, looking into his pools of blue. "You would do that for me? You said you haven't really told anyone."

He lifts a hand to my cheek. "But I would for you."

I kiss him softly and lean against him, nestling my nose onto his neck. "What am I going to do, Logan? What if they come after me?"

Logan leans away so he can look in my eyes and drops his brow a bit with just a shadow of a smile on his face. "We fight, of course." He shakes his head as if the answer were obvious and I should have known. *I suppose I should by now.*

In the morning I tell my dad that I have asked Logan to go with me to Boston for the day. The news greatly relieves his anxiety about me driving over two hours on my own to a place I have only been to a handful of times. Logan pulls up just as my dad and Liz are leaving to go to the rink. I see the exhaustion on their faces and can only imagine how they are looking forward to the end of the day.

My dad gives Logan a speech about driving carefully and his only daughter, blah, blah, blah. Logan takes it in stride, agreeing with my father and even making him feel better about me going.

"You do pretty well with dads. Got a lot of experience?"

"Hardly. I was always afraid that I would freak someone out if they knew. It wasn't hard to keep from friends and such, but keeping it from a girlfriend would be much harder because of the intimacy. As it is, I have to control myself around you because I still don't know if I can transfer other emotions beside the calm. Especially, to someone who's powers are as strong as yours."

"And what emotions have you been keeping from me, Mr. Blackwell?" I raise my eyebrow at him.

"Oh, no, you're not getting that information that easily."

I cross my arms in front of me and pout as he lets out a chuckle.

The rest of the drive is spent in random conversation and

debates about which hockey teams should have won the Stanley cup. It's not until we get within a few miles of Evangeline's home that the tension and anxiety begin to build.

"Do you want me to go with you to see her?"

I nod my head as I look around the neighborhood. All old brick homes, one story built closely together.

You have arrived at your destination. The kind voice on the GPS breaks the silence that had taken over.

The GPS on my phone indicates a brick house, not unlike the others in style, save for a covered porch that houses two rocking chairs. Logan parks the car along the street.

I look at Logan and he doesn't say a word. He simply leans forward, giving me a soft kiss and a nod.

We both slide out of the car at the same time, but I wait for Logan to round the car and take my hand. I walk up to the white wooden fence with the fading paint and unlatch it, letting us onto the walkway. We close the gate behind us and walk along a well-kept stone path lined with small, colorful flowers. We arrive at the first of three brick steps that lead up to the covered porch. We take each step at the same time and I glance at the rocking chairs before knocking on the door. They are classic wooden rocking chairs, varnished with some wear along the edges of the wood, between them, a small wooden table.

We open the screen door with the wooden frame and just

as I lift my hand to knock, I hear a voice come through the large wooden door.

"Come in Katelyn… and Logan." I stare at Logan with my eyes wide and wonder what the hell we have gotten ourselves into. Logan squeezes my hand as he shrugs his shoulders.

As we walk in I am stopped dead in my tracks. The woman before me looks only a bit older than my mother was when she had me and is almost the spitting image of my mother herself.

Sensing my unease, Logan puts his arm around me.

"Evangeline?" I ask, inching forward.

She smiles and tilts her head, her dark brown curls falling off her shoulder. When she smiles, the laugh lines tell more of her age, but not much.

"You, you don't look any different than when I last saw you, over ten years ago… How…"

Evangeline steps forward, putting her hands out for an embrace. "I am sure there are many questions that you have for me." She smiles and tilts her head. "But, all in due time."

I walk into her arms giving a cautious hug and then quickly make my way back to Logan's side. He extends his hand to her and I can tell he is trying to read her as she shakes his hand in return.

"Let me get you both something to drink. It has been a

long drive for you. Tea?"

Logan and I both nod before she disappears into the next room. The house is decorated in earthly tones and colors and I wonder if that is an indication to any powers she may have. To our right are a sofa with a flower pattern, a small wooden coffee table with carvings along the edges, and two mismatched chairs sitting in front of it. Along the far wall there is a tan brick fireplace with a white mantle. To our left is an oak dining table for four. It has some filigree carvings along its oval edges, but is otherwise plain, save for the fresh flower arrangement sitting in a glass cylinder. The seats around the table seem to be part of a set, with two others sitting in far ends of the room with a china cabinet in the center.

Evangeline walks back into the room with a tray and places it on the coffee table.

"I brought creamer and sugar because I wasn't sure how you took it."

"Thank you." I walked ahead, making our way around the chairs and to the sofa as Evangeline settles herself in a seat across from us.

"You are the spitting image of your mother." She tells me with a wide smile. "I loved her like my own you know. I could never have any of my own. Makes for a longer life when you are immortal."

I pinch my brow and widen my eyes.

Evangeline quickly jumps in. "Oh! Goodness, I didn't mean to frighten you. You aren't immortal, Kate, your mother's parents were a Langley and a mortal. My father fell in love with a Keeper of the Balance over a century ago. I was their only child, and as such inherited my mother's immortality. Your grandmother, my cousin, always called me her sister, so your mother knew me as her aunt." She takes a sip of her tea. "My apologies, I didn't mean to frighten you."

"It's alright." I shake off the near heart attack. "Do you have the same powers my mother had?"

"No, because of who my mother was, I inherited some elemental power from my father, but mostly the Keeper connection from my mother. That is how I knew you were coming and once you were at the door, that Logan was with you." She takes another sip. "But I did help your mother with her powers. She had mishaps when she was growing up that separated her from other children, but she pressed on. It wasn't until she met your father that she kept her powers at a minimum. I suspect your father knew to a certain degree, but never asked or judged. When you were younger, I sensed a great strength within you, as did Gamaliel. I wanted to be close to you, to help you, but I was also afraid that with the two of us in the same place, they would find you more quickly."

"So you know about them." I add cream and sugar to my

tea and try to keep Evangeline and Logan from seeing my shaky hand as I stir.

"I do." She dropped her gaze. "I can feel your energy, Katelyn. It would not surprise me if they can too, and if they are close to finding you."

"Did my mother's powers or energies… I don't know… emanate, I guess… the way mine do?"

"No." Evangeline shook her head with a smile. "I've yet to meet a witch whose powers match yours. I am willing to bet it has been a little difficult as of late. Perhaps, hard to control? Running with emotions?"

I take Logan's hand and squeeze. He looks at me and smiles.

"Logan carries quite the energy also." Evangeline raises her eyebrow and smirks as if she knows that we don't know this. "I have the feeling though, that he avoids exploring his powers if he does not need to."

I see Logan blush under the dim light of the room as he clears his throat and I give his hand a reassuring squeeze. When I do, I suddenly feel the nervousness inside him. I whip my head around to meet his gaze and he gives me a smirk. *So he can share more than the calm.*

"How am I supposed to take on a whole family?"

Evangeline's face changed suddenly with her brow pinching and her smile dropping. "Katelyn, do not give yourself the impression you will be taking on a family, or there could be much needless death. Not everyone from that family is hunting you. It is a handful, a small group dedicated to the task, some likely may not even be related to the Blackbournes. Remember, power attracts many. I would not be surprised if most of the family does not even know."

"How am I to know?" I release Logan's hand and rub my face.

"I am sure those who mean to hurt you will eventually make themselves seen. But your curse runs deep, do not let yourself be blinded by the past, by the emotions with which the initial curse was placed, or the powers that emerge. "

She puts up a finger and closes her eyes for a moment. "Just be sure that you understand what all this means. Your father, your stepmother, Logan, they are all targets. They may not come after you directly if they think you already have control over your powers."

"I know." I clasp my hands, dropping them into my lap and Logan slides over on the couch, putting his arms around me. As soon as he does, a light wave of calm makes its way through me.

Seemingly reading our movements, Evangeline smiles. "It is destiny that you two are together." She says with a smile as she puts her tea cup back on the tray and rests her hands in her lap.

"I will begin to ask any other witches I know if there is any news, or something strange going on that may lead to us finding them before they find you. I will keep in close contact with Gamaliel who I am sure is doing the same."

"Thank you." I stand from the sofa and Logan quickly follows.

I walk around to the foyer to make my way out of the house and Evangeline moves in front of me, her eyes filled with tears. "Must you go already?"

"I don't want my father to worry. He... he doesn't know I'm here," I say lowly, hoping I'm not offending her.

"I understand." Her tone is still sweet. She reaches out a shaky hand, scooping a set of wavy tresses that had fallen over my shoulder and lightly runs her hand beneath it. Her chin shakes lightly before she speaks. "You really are the mirror image of your mother. I miss her every day, as I miss you. Please," she presses her lips and keeps the tears from falling. "come see me again?" Her voice shook as she finished her small but meaningful request and it dawns on me how lonely she must be with almost all of our family having been killed or dying during childbirth. As if by a new instinct, I rush forward and gather her in my arms. This woman who I barely remember, but feel such a connection to, this woman who has been waiting patiently for me to come to her.

Logan moves to stand behind her, beaming a smile at me.

I release my great aunt and look into her green eyes, realizing they are almost identical to my mother's. "I promise."

She takes my face in her hands and leans it down, pressing her lips to my forehead and an unconscious smile makes its way across my face as she releases me and we make our way out of the quaint brick home.

"So, I'm curious..." Logan starts as I click on my seatbelt and he pulls away from the curb. "When was the last time, you reacted like that to anyone?"

I pout my lower lip and scrunch my nose a bit. "I can't remember." I smile now, looking at the home in my side view mirror as we drive away. "But it felt really good."

Logan reaches over and grabs my hand, placing a kiss on the back. He doesn't say a word, but I feel the pride he has for me and I like it. I know it's taking so much for him to allow me to feel these things from him. "So, where to now?" His blue eyes sparkle and the corner of his lip rises.

"Well, I suppose we should stop at Harvard so that I am not completely lying to my dad. Too bad it's not hockey season or we could have stopped for a Bruins game."

Logan huffs and scrunches his nose. "Um, you mean, we would make a trip to New York and watch the Rangers."

"Ew, the Rangers?" I fake sounds of vomiting.

"Um, yeah, lived in NY remember?"

"Yeah, we'll have to fix that, city boy," I laugh as Logan

chuckles and shakes his head.

"Anything else you'd like to change while you're at it? Geez…" He raises an eyebrow and smiles, his gorgeous white teeth gleaming like a damn toothpaste commercial and I catch the start of stubble making its way on his cheeks.

A smile creeps along my face slowly as I admire him. "No. I wouldn't change anything else… ever." I lean over the console placing a soft kiss on his cheek.

We spend most of the rest of the day on the Harvard campus taking in its enormity and even stopping at the gift shop where Logan buys shirts for dad, Liz and me, and even one for himself. I practically beg him not to do it and spend that money on us, but he pretends he can't hear me, so I eventually give in and stand there as he signs the receipt.

"So," Logan starts as he merges onto the highway on our way home "have you decided if you want to come to dinner on Friday and meet my dad?"

I gulp down the sudden lump in my throat. "Babe, I will meet whomever you want me to meet, but should I be prepared or something? I mean you didn't make him out to be the warmest guy in the world."

Logan chuckles, "I suppose you're right, and no, he's not the warmest, but he's not mean either. He's just a pain in my ass when it comes to business and his companies."

"Why is that?" I cross my legs and lean onto the center

console.

Logan sighs and his eyes stare ahead, his lips have dropped almost to a frown. "Well, I've always known that Erebos was a partner of sorts with my dad, but he wasn't really around much a few years ago, so I assumed he was a silent partner." He sets his chiseled jaw. "But lately, he has been showing up to more meetings, having more private meetings with my dad, and I just don't like him being around so much. To be honest, that is the main reason that my dad and I are at odds right now. He wants me to get more involved, but I keep telling him that I refuse unless he can basically put a leash on Erebos."

"Aaand, what did your dad say to that?" I ask lowly.

He moves his jaw back and forth before starting and steals a glance at me. "He was disappointed. I could tell that I hurt him when I told him I wouldn't. He's worked hard to build the life that he has for my mom and myself. But, I just can't... I won't. Not with Erebos trying to call the shots."

I put my hand on Logan's cheek and he leans into me. I feel the anxiety in him. "I wish I can give you some of my calm."

He turns his head and smiles. "You are all the calm I need."

I feel a blush creep up, but I don't try to hide it or stop it. "Maybe you should do some detective work and see what position it is exactly that Erebos holds and how you and/or, your dad can keep him from trying to be so influential."

Logan gives a wicked smile. "That's not a bad idea, Angel." He nods his head. "Not bad at all... though, if he really is a partner of sorts, I might be screwed."

"We'll cross that bridge when we get to it, baby." I slide my hand beneath his and rest it on his leg.

"We?" He raises his eyebrow at me.

I feel my heart beat hard against my chest. "Yes, we. If you think for one moment that this is going to be a one way street of you doing things for me, helping me and me just sitting by and watching when something is going on in your life then you have another thing coming."

"Wow, she decides to embrace her powers and now she just thinks she is going to boss everyone around," he says, shaking his head and ending with "Pfft."

I giggle and playfully slap his arm before pulling out my phone to text my dad and let him know we are on our way back. I play with the thought of telling him that I went to see my aunt, but I realize that it will incite more questions than I am willing to answer right now. To be honest, the less they know about me at the moment, the better. Maybe they will be of less use to someone who is looking for me. I click send and clench my teeth together as the thought of something happening to Dad or Liz drops stones in my stomach.

CHAPTER II

I am plagued for the fourth night in a row this week with nightmares of a mysterious figure chasing me through the streets of Penhale, my bare feet splashing through puddles of blood belonging to my ancestors. I try to fight, but my powers are useless, as if they are neutralized and I am forced to watch as the figure kills Logan and my parents.

I jolt upright in my bed to find my camisole stuck to my chest and back. I wipe my face of the sweat to find tears as well. I pick my phone up off the nightstand. Five fifty five. *Great. I will get to meet Logan's dad with enough bags under my eyes for a trip to Paris.* I consider texting him, but I don't want to wake him. The pull to be in his arms creates a pain in my chest that resonates through my body. I think back to the conversation I had with my dad before going to bed. He was standing in his new Harvard University shirt, telling me how much of a difference he has seen in me and how happy he is to see me with Logan. He asked if I had any 'incidents' and I couldn't stand lying to him completely so I just told him that they were small and that I think I can control them now. It wasn't a complete lie, but it turned my stomach all the same and I make a vow as he walks away to tell him about everything I have found out as soon as I can.

I get up to get some water in the bathroom and on my way back I walk over to the window, pulling the curtains back to peer outside. The morning sun's rays have begun to pour onto our front yard and driveway through the large trees along the fence, but the morning dreariness still lingers in the shadows. I catch a glimpse of sunlight reflecting off something in the distance, but I am blocked by the sycamore trees along the fence.

I squat down in front of the window and peer beneath the lower branches and see that the sunlight is gleaming off the rim of a large tire. Practically pressing my face onto my windowsill, I catch the bottom of the frame of the vehicle, gunmetal grey. It has been days since I last saw it following Logan and I to the coffee shop, then disappearing again. I drop onto my knees and clench my teeth, angered by the fact that I do not know who this is, or what they want. I consider trying to use my powers to start a storm or a fire since I had been practicing, but decide not to in case that is exactly what they are wanting. For me to prove who I am. I crawl back into bed, but I stare at the ceiling, getting up every twenty minutes or so to check on the vehicle. It isn't until just before my dad and Liz leave to go to the rink at nine that it pulls away.

I finally decide to get up and jump in the shower as I begin to mentally prepare myself for dinner tonight. I call Logan after my shower and fill him in on everything that happened in my nightmare and this morning, and just as I thought he would he asks me why I didn't call him.

"Because I didn't want to wake you."

"Kate-," he starts, but I don't I don't let him finish.

"I know, I know, not a good enough excuse."

"Not for something that important." There is no playfulness in his voice.

I smile about his concern for me. "So, when will we be finding out more about Mr. Primordial Evil?"

Logan laughs hard breaking the solemnness I was picking up in his voice. "I want to speak to my dad today and see what information I can get without raising questions."

"Sounds good."

"What will you be doing today?"

"Not much. Maybe hang out at the house, do my nails,

organize my closet, make some plans to meet friends, you know, like most girls. Oh, and I need to remember to practice the magical abilities that have been intensifying in the hopes of destroying the person who is trying to kill me." I shrug my shoulders as if he could see me. "No big deal."

Hearing Logan's laugh pulls a giggle out of me.

"Yup, just another day in the life of Katelyn Miller." He makes a grunting sound and I wonder if he is sitting himself up in the bed. "Alright, Miss No Big Deal, I will try and get that conversation going with my dad and I will see you later."

"Okay, see you later." I push the 'end' button on my phone and let out a small sigh.

I spend most of the afternoon attempting to distract myself from the butterflies that have by now officially nested in my stomach by practicing my magic. I begin to contemplate how I can test whether or not I have any abilities that have to do with the mind, but I haven't a clue. I pull out my phone and text Gamaliel and he is at my house in minutes. I begin to believe he uses portals more often than he lets on.

"I was just about to call you."

"Have you found something out?"

"Possibly. Regarding the SUV that you texted me about earlier in the week. I should be hearing something within the next few days." Gamaliel makes his way over to one of the wicker seats on the porch and dusts off the tan cushion before sitting down. "So, how can I help you?"

Though he is wearing a ball cap, I can see that he cut his hair and his casual dress of jeans and a t-shirt are starting to grow on me. He definitely doesn't creep me out the way he used to. "How do I know if I have any abilities regarding the mind? I mean, I know I can block people out, but can I know what someone else is thinking?"

Gamaliel furrows his brow. "Katelyn, those powers can be dangerous. They are tempting in ways you cannot imagine and can lead to corruption or insanity."

Wow, I never thought of it like that. "Oh."

"I just... I wanted to have a leg up if I see Erebos again." I sit in an identical chair opposite him, across from the matching table with the glass top. "I was hoping that maybe if I could, I can also stop those headaches I get when he tries to read me."

"Hm." Gamaliel leans forward onto his elbows. "I am unsure how to counter that since that is due to your ability to keep him out." He squints his eyes at me. "Try to read my thoughts. I will try to not block you out, though it happens naturally to me by now."

"How do I do that?"

"Just picture my mind as a building of sorts... make your way through the front doors and start walking down hallways until you see doors you can peer into." He laughs at my scrunched nose. "It doesn't have to be exactly like that, but you need to have a visual of you getting to the thoughts…. Hallways, passages, whatever the method, you need to see it happening. Do you understand?"

"I think so." I bite the inside of my lip and lock gazes with him. My mind begins to wander and though I am looking right at him, I see myself standing at a door. It's black and there is no knob, but if I push, it gives way. I begin to ease myself inside, but the darkness surrounds me and I cannot see anything. My head begins to hurt so I break my concentration and look away.

"Are you alright?" Gamaliel leans back in his seat.

"My head started to hurt so I stopped."

"My apologies." He shrugs his shoulders slightly. "It is very difficult for me to allow anyone in my thoughts. My desire to protect my mind and thoughts is instinctual. The pain was me, fighting back." He cocks his head to the side. "Were you able to see anything at all?"

"I made it through a door. But it was all dark."

Gamaliel nods his head and smirks. "You've made it further than anyone else. Most cannot get past the door." He stands and begins pacing the length of my porch, lightly hitting the pillars he passes with his hand. "You must try to ignore the pain you feel. If you can somewhat zone it out and keep calm, you may be able to progress further, or at the very least, defend yourself without hurting." He begins to walk out into my yard and turns, "I will contact you as soon as I have information. Be careful."

I nod my head and he turns again, walking until he disappears in between the trees.

Later in the afternoon, I pull into Logan's driveway and ease my Jeep into the parking space next to his Tahoe. I try to gulp down the lump in my throat, but in the past hour it's become a permanent fixture, joining the butterflies in my stomach. At this point, I think I should consider myself lucky if I don't puke all over Mr. Blackwell. Logan told me not to be nervous, but I realize that it's not so much meeting his dad, but being in his house that has me on edge since this is where I last saw Erebos and I would rather not run into him again anytime this century if I could possibly help it.

I step out of the Jeep and close the door, catching my reflection. I question quickly whether or not my tan spaghetti strap satin draping top is too revealing, but realize that on top of the fact that it's too late to change, it's also too hot. I smooth my hands over my dark denims and look down at my brown strappy three inch heels, happy that I was able to give myself a quick pedicure today. I drape my brown purse over my shoulder, flip my hair a little, filling my layered waves with some volume and turn to walk to the house when my heart drops.

"Geez!" I yell, falling back and bracing myself against my Jeep with one hand while the other is planted firmly on my heaving chest.

Logan laughs hard and makes his way to me.

"How long have you been there?" I breathe, trying to slow my heart rate.

"From about the time you closed the door and nervously checked yourself out," he says between chuckles.

"Well, I am so glad that I can amuse you!" I walk over and jokingly swing my purse at him, but he jumps out of the way.

He reaches over and puts an arm around my waist as I shoulder my purse again, still smiling wide. "You look amazing."

"Yeah?" I quickly question as I wrinkle my nose and purse my lips.

"Yeah," he says as he lowers his lips to mine, and leans me up against the Jeep. "Hm. I'm tempted to keep you to myself tonight."

I smile against his lips. "I like that idea." I pull my head back and look him over. His dark hair is combed back and held in place by what I'm sure is a pomade or something since it doesn't look wet, the blue in his eyes is almost as dark as the rim, and I'm thinking it's due to him being nervous about tonight as well. I bring my hands up to his face and feel the stubble beneath it as I bite my lip. "I like this," I say, slowly running my hands along his structured jaw, feeling the growth against my skin.

"Mmm," is all he can get out before pressing his lips to mine, this time with more desire, as his hands squeeze my hips. He stops, putting his forehead to mine. "We should get inside." I can see in his face he really doesn't want to. I can't blame him. I'd be the first to offer to jump in the Jeep and drive away right now.

I run my finger along his lip, removing traces of my lipstick, and then pull out my compact to check my makeup before going in.

As soon as I walk through the door, Sabina is walking towards me with her arms open wide. I smile and immediately wrap my arms around her for a quick hug. It still feels strange, opening up like this and letting people close to me, but it's slowly growing on me.

"I am so glad you came tonight. Logan's father is very excited to meet you," she beams. Her dark hair is pulled into a messy bun and her makeup is minimal, though she could pass for a model. *Seriously, this family is genetically blessed.*

Logan takes my hand as his mother turns around and leads the way into the dining room. We walk into the formal dining room and immediately I feel as though I am taken into one of my books that takes place in the eighteen hundreds. A large oval dark cherry wood table sits in the center on an intricately patterned rug, with matching chairs surrounding it. The wallpaper alternates two beige colored stripes until they reach the white chair rail in the center of the room then a dark burgundy color fills the lower half. Every window in the room is draped with elegant heavy draperies, allowing for the only light in the room to come from the beautiful crystal and silver chandelier. The china cabinet takes up almost the entire length of the wall, while the matching thin buffet table sits nestled between the two large windows. A large mirror with a four inch Victorian frame sits on the far wall over the larger buffet table with a marble top.

"Dinner should be ready in just a moment, and Logan's father should be joining us-" Sabina's face lights up as she stops mid-sentence and smiles at her husband across the room. "Well, now, I suppose," she finishes with a light laugh.

I turn my attention to the doorway and see what I am sure Logan is going to look like in about twenty or so years, since he is the spitting image of him, except for the green eyes. My heart begins to race and I wonder if Logan can feel it while he holds my hand.

"So this is the young lady I have been hearing so much about." He tilts his head and smiles, but there is a seriousness behind it.

I step forward, releasing Logan's hand and approach his

dad. "Yes, sir. I am Katelyn Miller. It's a pleasure to meet you, Mr. Blackwell." I extend my hand and he slides his in, giving a firm shake. For a moment I find myself hoping that he doesn't have the same power as Logan or he would know that I am a nervous wreck right now.

Mr. Blackwell looks me over and extends his hand toward the table, for us to sit. Logan pulls out my chair and I thank God that he has decided to sit between his father and myself while his mother sits at the other end of the table, closest to me.

"So, Katelyn," Mr. Blackwell begins "have you lived here long?"

Harrison walks in, placing a plate of salad in front of me along with a glass of water.

"Yes, sir. Not always in Cove though, we lived in New Hartford until I was about four."

"I am beginning to like it, though I suppose I am too used to the city," he says before starting on his salad.

We make it through the meal of lobster bisque, braised beef short ribs, and baked potato, keeping the conversation to family and work. Though I am sure I have never answered so many questions about myself or my dad's work. Mr. Blackwell remains pleasant for the most part, but begins to anger when he starts on the subject of wanting Logan to do more work in his company or even in the office he will be opening in Stamford. Luckily, Sabina intervened and put out the fire before it got out of control.

Harrison walks in with a serving cart upon which there are four small round white dishes with what I am sure is crème brulee. Just as he is placing the plates on the table, I get an ominous feeling and turn to the doorway, but it is empty. Not even a moment later, Erebos walks in.

"Oh, my apologies, I did not mean to interrupt your dinner."

Mr. Blackwell remains irrelevant as if this has happened before, but Sabina shoots daggers at him with her eyes.

Erebos glares at me, giving an evil smirk before turning his attention back to Logan's dad. "Well, since you and your son are both here, perhaps we can have a quick meeting regarding the branch we will be opening here in Stamford."

Before Mr. Blackwell can respond, Logan starts, "I have plans with Katelyn after dinner."

As soon as he is done, Mr. Blackwell sets his jaw as he finishes his dessert, shooting an irritated glare at his son.

I lean over slightly toward Logan. "I don't mind waiting for you."

Logan stands quickly. "Will you excuse us?" he asks his mother and father who quickly nod in agreement.

He takes my hand and pulls me to the other side of the room and out the door that Harrison had been coming in through all evening, leading me into a hallway.

"Angel, I don't want him around you any more than you want to be around him." Logan begins as he paces the hallway.

"I know, but this might help us start getting the information we need regarding Mr. Creepy and his involvement with your dad."

Logan chuckles at my new nickname for Erebos and sighs, twisting the corner of his mouth. "Fine. But I will keep it short."

"Fine by me." I plant a soft kiss on his lips and we re-enter the dining room, "Be careful with Erebos. Try to keep your mind closed to him, "I whisper just as we stop near his mother's seat.

"Father." Mr. Blackwell sits back in his chair, folding his arms across his chest. "I will stay and hear what you have to say." He shoots a hateful glare at Erebos.

Logan's father gives a genuine smile and looks at me, nodding his head. "Very well, son."

They all stand and leave to the den which I am told is across the hall. Sabina decides that she does not want to join them and asks if I would mind excusing her as she has to ensure that she has some paperwork together for the new office they are opening. She tells me that I can wait wherever I would like and that I should make myself at home.

I take her up on the offer to make myself at home and begin

to explore the enormous house, eventually making my way upstairs. I find myself continually fiddling with the locket around my neck as I walk from room to room. I am amazed at how she has made use of all the rooms. I continue to explore and so far have found a gym, a craft room stocked so well, that it rivals the nearby craft stores, a couple of guest bedrooms and another office.

I walk in to look at the books on the shelf in the small office when I hear the door slam behind me. Erebos stands in front of it, his lips pull into a thin line and his grey eyes squint slightly. I reach down to my pocket and realize that my phone is in my purse in the coat closet downstairs.

I feel my chest rising and falling hard as he slowly steps forward.

"Do you believe that you can fool me?" He lunges forward putting his hand on my neck and lifting me slightly off the ground and into the bookcase behind me, causing several books to fall to the ground. I grab at his wrist trying to make him release me, but his grip is too tight. He leans forward getting close to my neck and I cringe, trying to pull out of his way. He takes a deep breath, "I know who you are. I can feel it coming off of you. I can smell it on you."

"I don't know what you're talking about, you psychotic bastard," I manage to get out between chokes.

He chuckles, "Is that the game we are going to play?" He

stares at me and I feel him trying to enter my mind. Searing pains shoot through my head and I try to focus as Gamaliel told me. I glare back at him and picture myself getting into his thoughts as his eyes go wide. I see a dark door, just as I did with Gamaliel and I force my way in. Once in, I see flashes of offices, of Logan and his family, of me and my family, and suddenly it all goes black as he increases the pressure on my neck, my concentration shattered. "You don't want to play in there, little one. It's a dangerous place to be. You may be fooling Logan, and his parents may be oblivious to you and even to me, but you don't fool me at all." His breath lingers hot on my face.

My eyes begin to water as I bring my arm down hard onto his, loosening his grip on me just enough to escape and gasp for the air my lungs are begging me for. "You can play dumb all you want, but if you are who I think you are..." he chuckles again and my stomach turns. "I will make you watch as I kill your family first, then Logan, and then you."

"If you so much as touch my family or Logan, I will hunt you down and kill you," I spit out the words as I find my way onto my feet.

He backs up slowly to the door. "Maybe I will start with your aunt in Salem." He cocks his head, "Oh, and if you think of telling your boyfriend about our little encounter, I won't wait to see if you are in fact, *the one*. Understand?" he finishes as he opens the door and walks out into the hallway.

I run out behind him but he is gone. I look down the hallway and see the familiar door. Quickly, I make my way down the hall and into Logan's room, shutting the door behind me and leaning against it.

"Angel!" Logan runs in from the balcony. "Where have you been? I was loo-" he stops as he approaches, taking in my appearance.

I bring my hand up to my neck as tears start streaming down my face.

"What the hell happened? It looks like..." he drops off and takes my face in his hands. "I'll kill him. I swear I'll kill him." He starts to make his way to the door, but I grab his hand and yank him back.

"No," I say through choked sobs. "He already has an idea that I'm the one. He says it's just a matter of time before he can prove it. I... I think he just wanted me to admit it, or use my powers, but I didn't. He said if I say anything to you that he won't wait. He will kill my parents, you and then me." Logan begins to walk me over to his sofa when there is a knock on the door and Erebos calls to him from the other side.

I see the rage in Logan's eyes and shake my head. "I'll wait in your bedroom. See what he has to say." I rush to the other side of the room and push the door forward.

"What is it Erebos?" I hear Logan give an aloof tone as

Erebos lets himself in.

"Where is Katelyn?" he asks, though I suspect he knows.

"I think she is with my mother in her office. I haven't seen her since before our meeting... Why?"

I hear Erebos pacing the room and I can already picture his hostile and critical grin. "Really?"

He stops near the bedroom door and I make my way over to Logan's queen size bed, slowly lowering myself onto the floor and squeezing underneath it. I see the light pour in as he opens the door and almost immediately Logan is standing behind him.

"Is there any reason you are searching my room for my girlfriend?"

"Your girlfriend," he starts. "is quite special, isn't she?"

I watch as their feet get farther and farther from the bedroom door and breathe a sigh of relief.

"Yes. She is."

"I would even venture to say unique. Kind of like you?" He stops pacing. His condescending tone has me clenching my teeth.

"What the hell are you getting at Erebos?"

"Don't play stupid with me, Logan. I am well aware of your powers and that they are likely twice as strong as your father's."

"I know what you are doing to my father." I see Logan get

closer to Erebos until they are almost toe to toe. "I saw it in the meeting. He can't keep you out the way I can and-"

"And the way your girlfriend can?" he interrupts. "You need to think about whose side you are really on Logan. The first of likely many relationships? Or your blood? She's not who you think she is, Logan. She is a danger to our kind and to our family. When she finds out who you are, she will turn on you."

"Get out," I hear Logan speak through gritted teeth.

Erebos simply chuckles lowly and begins to make his way out of the room. As soon as the door closes and I hear the lock, I slide out from underneath the bed.

"I can definitely say I never thought I would be doing that," I say as I give Logan my hand and he helps me up.

He pulls me into a tight embrace. "We have to figure out what the hell his plan or angle is, and how to stop him."

"What do you mean his plan or angle?" I pull back and furrow my brow.

He lets me go and sits on the edge of his bed, rubbing his chin. "Think about it. If he thought it was you, why not just kill you and be done with it? Why risk it? What is he waiting for?" He stands quickly. "We need to talk to Gamaliel. We need more information about the Blackbournes. There has to be something we are missing." He stands and turns toward the door, but I grab his arm and turn him gently to me.

"Why did he say that if I find out who you are, I'll turn on you?"

Logan sighs and looks at me. "I'd be lying if I say that I hadn't thought about this part of the legend... If Erebos is truly a Blackbourne, then that means I am too, and you are to take revenge on the family who slaughtered your ancestors."

My eyes watered. "But you heard Evangeline! Not all of you are like him."

"I know we aren't. But didn't you notice the way she said that? Like you may or may not have control over yourself when the time comes." He shakes his head. "I don't know, it doesn't matter anyway."

"It doesn't matter? It does matter! I will not hurt you. You aren't like Erebos and I know that. I don't care how strong my powers are or will become, I know who you are, I know how you feel, and how I feel about you."

Logan pulls me in and holds me tight against him. "I know baby, I know," he says onto my head and follows it with a kiss.

I text Gamaliel and ask him to meet us. I also call my great aunt and explain to her that we are looking for a trigger, or something that will indicate what Erebos is waiting on. Logan and I make our way downstairs and find his parents in the living room, having just said their goodbyes to Erebos. We say our own quick goodbye and rush out to my car in an attempt to follow him.

"What kind of car is he driving?" I ask as Logan pulls up to the first stoplight.

"Today? That one." He nudges his head toward a silver four door Cadillac two blocks down at a stop sign. "Luckily we are in an area with few ways out."

We tail him for almost an hour and end up following Erebos to a small colonial house in Westchester, New York. The home is small in comparison to its surrounding neighbors, but sits on easily six or seven acres of land.

"I have a funny feeling that we might find out more about Erebos and his plans here than at my dad's offices."

"I agree," I say as I peer through the window, trying to glimpse through the trees. "Though, we have no idea how long we will have to wait before we can get in there," I finish, leaning back in my chair as I lose sight of Erebos's feet behind another tree.

"Leave that to me. My dad will be home all weekend, so if I can convince him that I am interested in speaking with him more about work, I can probably get more information about where Erebos will be and when." Logan pulls off the curb and continues down the street, taking us back to Shippan.

"I've never tried to break into anyone's house, and I'm guessing you haven't either, so we will have to figure out how we are getting in," Logan chuckles as we get on the highway.

"I'm sure we can figure something out." I say, chewing on my lip, hoping I will be able to think of a way in.

Halfway home, I get a text from Gamliel saying that he will be waiting on us to meet with him and that he has news regarding the gunmetal grey SUV.

"Of course!" I say slamming my forehead into my palm. "That is how we can do this."

"What? Do what?" Logan looks at me with his brows pinched.

"Gamaliel! He can create portals. I don't know if he'd be okay to use them for breaking and entering, but it's worth a shot to ask him."

"Portals?" Logan raises an eyebrow.

I let out a sigh. "There is one more thing that I need to tell you... not because I was trying to keep it from you, but because I figured I was already putting so much magic and crazy things on you already."

Keeping his eyebrow raised, he twists his mouth to the side. "Ooookay. Lay it on me."

"The day you went to look for me in the park, I did meet with Gamaliel, like I told you, and he did inform me about my past and all that. There is just one thing that I had to ask about and have him explain so, he had to show me." I look at Logan, waiting for a change in his expression, but the only change is that his mouth is now almost a thin line. I sigh before continuing. "Remember when I was missing and I told you that I thought I was in a house?"

"Yeah."

"I really was. I was in his house. He made some tea to clear my head and tried telling me I had powers. That went over like a lead balloon and I decided to get the heck out of there. When I opened the door, I was back in the woods and his house was nowhere to be found. On my birthday I asked him how that was possible and he showed me. He said that very few beings are able to make portals. Usually Keepers of the Balance and of course, angels, and the fallen the demons. He made one and took me through it."

"So, someone makes a portal and you just hop right in?" Logan shakes his head. "What have I gotten myself into?" He lets out a sigh, "well, at least it's never going to be boring," he ends with a slight chuckle.

I drop my brows and give a sarcastic smile.

"Anyway... I ended up in a forest in England. It's the same forest where my ancestors were buried. I don't know how, but I ended up walking straight to the burial site and as if I was there, I saw the events of that night."

"That must have been kind of scary." The sarcastic tone was gone and I can tell he really meant what he was saying.

"It was. It hurt to see it all. It was almost as if I felt some of their pain. It was so weird." I look down at my hands in my lap. "I'm sorry I didn't tell you about that before. I just… I know you're really understanding and have yet to have me committed, but I figured I just couldn't freak you out all at once. I mean, most people go into a relationship and have date nights, movie time, a frolic on a beach, and make out while just hanging out, and I'm dragging you to meet my half-witch, half-keeper aunt, forcing you to find out information about a psycho family member and keep an ass ton of secrets for me," I stop my rambling, still staring at my hands.

"A frolic on a beach?" Logan asks in his most serious tone.

I look up at him and he's smiling at me, causing me to burst into a fit of laughter. "Well, you know what I meant." I say between laughs.

Logan takes a hand from my lap and puts it to his lips. "I wouldn't want it any other way." He gives me a wicked smile. "And for the record, we do have make outs while hanging out and I quite enjoy them."

I feel the blush consume my body, but I don't turn away.

We meet Gamaliel at the coffee shop, this time sitting at a small table opposite where we usually sit in case the gunmetal grey SUV comes looking, they won't immediately see us.

"Are you serious?" Gamaliel folds his arms across his chest and leans back in a wooden seat.

"It will be quicker and cleaner than trying to…" I look around to ensure no one is listening, "trying to break a window or something."

He leans forward onto the table and takes his black coffee in his hands, staring at the liquid until it starts to spin on its own. "You do realize that I have never done this before and if I consider it now, it is only so we can finally put an end to this centuries old madness."

"Well, it's not like I will have other reasons to ever ask you again." I take a sip of my Chai and glance at Logan who has been silent for the most part.

"You will be sure that he will not be there?" Gamaliel sets his eyes on Logan.

"Yes. I can find out by tomorrow morning at the latest when we will be able to go."

"Fine," he gives in and takes a sip of the dark liquid bitterness in his cup. "We will meet where we made the portal last time." He lifts his eyes over the cup and looks at me as he drinks the rest. "Also, the gunmetal grey SUV that has been following you, belongs to a colleague of Erebos. It appears he has a small handful of people he has convinced to be loyal to his cause, since from what my informants have been able to gather, there are none left in the Blackbourne family who will support him."

"Why is that?" I ask, though I wouldn't want them actually supporting him.

"Throughout the centuries, there were many who sought

out forgiveness for what their ancestors did, thinking that they would somehow pay the price, or their children would. However, for a long time there were those who insisted on ensuring that no revenge would ever be taken on a Blackbourne." He turns the cup in his hands. "Pride covers a multitude of sins, it is said." On the third spin, the cup is filled again with black coffee. "Those Blackbournes saw to it to go after Langley daughters, kill Keepers so that they can keep their identities safe, and even go against other Blackbournes who opposed them. As you can imagine, the Keepers and Langleys were not too keen on this and were not content to sit back and allow it, so they took matters into their own hands, dwindling their numbers. Erebos is the last, since his own father died several years ago. It is said that his father left him all he will need to know regarding you and what he needs to do to secure the Blackbourne future and re-instate the name."

"And your informant is sure of this?"

"Yes. That is why I will agree to help you into his house."

"Thank you, Gamaliel." I look at him, sorry that we have to ask him to do this.

"I don't know. This is the first time this has ever happened, and magic evolves and de-evolves. I cannot guarantee what you are capable of or will do." he blurts out, prompting a questionable look from Logan.

"What?" I open my eyes wide and glance at Logan who is doing the same.

"Gamaliel, what are you talking about?" Logan puts his hands on the table in front of us.

"Just answering a question that Katelyn has been mulling over in her mind since I walked through the door. So much so, that I couldn't help but see it."

Logan turns his gaze on me, his eyes sad. "Are you afraid that you will hurt me?"

Gamaliel stands, drinking what is left of the coffee in his cup. "Goodnight, you two. I expect a call or text in the morning."

Logan flinches his gaze toward Gamaliel with a quick goodnight before focusing on me again. "Well?"

"Yes." I feel my eyes water and I bite my lip to keep the tears from falling.

"You have to defeat a raging psycho who has been hunting you his whole life, along with others of his family, master your own powers, figure out his agenda, and keep your parents safe and your biggest concern at the moment is whether or not you will hurt me?" He smiles until it reaches his eyes and wraps his arms around me, pulling me close until my head rests on his shoulder. "You really need to sort out your priorities," he says in his best British accent quoting my favorite book and movie series.

I laugh as he holds me, but despite what he says and the light mood he tries to create, there are still many more questions than answers.

CHAPTER 12

Noooo! I scream as I stare at their lifeless bodies. The grass around them is soaked in their blood that I am guilty of spilling. I drop to my knees as the trees surrounding me begin to spin, Erebos' laughter filling my ears. I take Logan's lifeless body in my arms and shake him, begging him to wake. When he doesn't, I put him down and crawl to my dad and Liz taking both their blood soaked hands in mine and putting them to my face, begging them to answer me, to move, to show some sign of life. I sob so hard, I feel nauseous. I stare at Gamaliel's body in the distance and Erebos walks up behind me.

"Do you see now, why you should not have these powers?"

My eyes glow blue and I feel a tingle in my hands. When I turn to face him, a blue light shoots out from my hands, blinding me and knocking us to the ground.

I wake up in a pool of sweat again and realize that at this rate, I may as well put benches in my room and call it a sauna. I sigh as I get up and grab a towel from my bathroom, throwing it on my bed. I lay on it and stare at the window, watching the rain drip down the glass through a crack between the curtains. I follow a single drop all the way down until it hits the outer frame and wonder if I can do it, if I can control the path I need to take in order to accomplish what I must. My thoughts are interrupted by the buzzing on my nightstand. I pick it up and wonder who could be texting me at six in the morning.

Logan – Can't sleep, figured you would be up.

Me – Nightmare… can't sleep either.

Logan – Wish I could help. Too bad you aren't here.

Me – Wish I was.

I smile and think of what it would be like to be lying next to him right now. How he would have wrapped his arms around me, despite the sweat to comfort me from my nightmare.

I call him because the desire to hear his voice is not satisfied with just reading his messages.

"Hey, Polo," I say in a whisper as he picks up the phone.

"Hey, Angel." His voice is low and a bit raspy and I want to crawl through the phone and into his lap.

"Sorry, I just wanted to hear your voice."

"Don't ever be sorry for that, baby." I hear a long yawn and picture him stretching, probably sleeping shirtless in his giant bed. "You should try and get more sleep though. Who knows what today will hold for us."

"I know. I will try in a few. I can hear my dad and Liz getting ready to leave. They told me last night that they are taking a few days off to recover from last weekend's craziness."

"Where are they going?"

"Martha's Vineyard. One of the skater's parents has a house there and told them they could stay a few days."

"That was nice of them."

"Yeah, it was." I try and think of what the plans might be today once we know Erebos' schedule, but my mind continues to wander to Logan.

"You ok? You're kind of quiet." His voice is still low and raspy and I feel like I should let him sleep, but I can't.

"Just wishing I was there with you."

"You and me both."

"Can I ask you something?"

"Anything."

"Do you sleep without a shirt?"

Logan chuckles and clears his throat. "Maybe you should come over and find out."

I picture the sarcastic grin on his face, probably putting one arm behind his head while he lays with his sheets down around his waist, and his other hand over his six pack. *Well hell, this is what most teenage girls think of when they aren't freaking out about powers, psychos, and family curses.* I feel the heat rise in my body and I bite my lip, unable to get the image of him out of my head. *Yep, I bet he is totally rocking some sexy bed head, too.*

"You have no idea how I would love to do that."

"We will have to arrange that then." His voice is less raspy and I realize that he is probably more awake.

"With this conversation, we are not going to get any rest at all," I laugh.

He chuckles, "I don't care about rest, I like where this conversation is headed. Besides, I haven't asked what you are wearing."

"Not so fast, Polo. You want to know, you'll have to be around one night to find out."

Logan laughs out loud. A sound I have grown to love. "Don't tempt me, Angel. You say that one more time and I will have to make it happen."

I laugh lowly and speak slowly "You'll ... have ... to ... be ... around ... one ... night ... to ... find ... out."

Logan chuckles again and this time it's low and sexy.

"And you expect me to go back to sleep now?"

I giggle.

"What time are your parents leaving?"

"In about an hour," I say warily.

"I'll be there in an hour and ten minutes."

"Oh no, you don't, Polo. You need to be there when your dad gets up so we can find out about his schedule and Erebos' too."

Logan groans. "can't I just call him from your house?"

"Um, I'm pretty sure that it won't work the same."

Logan sighs and groans at the same time making me laugh. "Fine, but this is far from over."

"I'm counting on it. Now go back to sleep for a bit."

"Right, like that'll happen." I hear him shifting in his bed.

"Logan?"

"Yea, babe?"

"N-Nothing. Never mind. I'll see you later."

"Okay. See you later."

I hang up and stare at his picture on my phone. *I hope I don't hurt him.*

After having the life scared out of me with my nightmare, I spend the rest of the morning practicing using my powers. I've managed to do well controlling elements, but I haven't had practice with the mind and that concerns me. I mean, yeah, I can try to strike him down with lightning or something, but that's not exactly an easy method. I try controlling the bursts of energy that seem to flow out of my hands, like the day I confronted Samantha, but it's nowhere near as powerful as it was that day and I begin to assume that it's fueled by emotions. *Shocker*.

I'm about to try it again when I hear the doorbell. I rush to the door knowing it's Logan and yank it open.

"Hey there, Po…" I drop off at first glance of him. His eyes are solemn and there is no trace of a smile. "Logan, what's wrong?"

He shakes his head. "Got the information and texted it to Gamaliel. We can go tonight; there is some function that Erebos has to be at."

I grab his hand and pull him in. "Um, that's nice and all, but what is wrong?"

Logan takes a ragged breath. "They found more lesions on my mom's MRI."

"Wha.. what are you talking about? Lesions of what?"

"My mom has MS."

"Wait, MS, as in Multiple Sclerosis? Why didn't you tell me?"

"Well, in my defense, there has been a lot going on. Plus, we thought that she had it under control with this new experimental medication she was on." I walk Logan over to my sofa where he buries his face in his hands.

"Well, can't we find a witch or someone who has healing

powers? Maybe they can…," I drop off when he shakes his head. "We tried. It doesn't work that way. Most of the healing we can do is superficial, or relative to emotions, for some it's only strictly for the earth. Healing on that scale is a miracle and only God has that power."

"Wait, *we* can do?" I slid two fingers under his chin and lift his face towards me. "Logan, I thought you said you can't heal others?"

"I can't, but I am considered a healer as well as those who can," he sighs and leans back. "I know I'm being over dramatic. I should be lucky that it's not something she will die from, just die with, but I know the pain it causes her and it hurts me to see her like that."

"You're not being dramatic. You're being a great son." I reach over, putting my arms around him and pulling him towards me until his head is on my chest and I am running my fingers through his hair. All this time I have been trying to solve my own problems and never once thought that he could be going through something. We sit like that for at least fifteen minutes in silence, just being there.

"Can I try something?"

Logan lifts his head and tilts it to the side as I take his hands in mine. "I know you can give your calm and happiness, but have you ever tried to take any from anyone?"

He gives a crooked smile. "No one has ever offered."

"I'm offering." I don't know if it's something I can do, but I try nonetheless to picture my own hope and calm going into him.

Logan closes his eyes and takes a deep breath. Pressing his hands against mine. We sit that way for a few minutes before he says anything. "For someone so cynical, you carry a lot of hope." He opens his eyes and smiles.

My heart leaps and I literally feel his emotions changing. "Logan." His name escapes my lips as he brings his hand to my cheek. He brushes his lips against mine and kisses them softly.

We spend the afternoon practicing my powers. Logan lets me try to enter his mind, but instead of just letting me, he fights back since I know it won't be that easy with Erebos. I manage to make it in, and even get a few flashes of his thoughts. Quite a bit were of us, one of which he shut me out of fast and I'm thinking it had to do with this morning's conversation because I thought I saw a blush creep across his face.

At eight o clock we jump in his car and head to the beach to meet Gamaliel. I had called and asked why we couldn't just make the portal in the forest behind my house, but he doesn't want to risk it, in case someone is home and tries following us through.

The beach has a few more cars than I would have thought

with couples walking along the walkways and shoreline. Gamaliel sits alone on the bench where we usually have our conversations.

My stomach is turning over on itself in fear of finding Erebos at his home. If he was willing to threaten us in Logan's home, I shudder to think what he would do in his own. We walk up to the bench and without turning around, Gamaliel acknowledges us. As we round the seat, he stands.

"Are you ready?" he asks solemnly.

"You do not seem very certain about wanting to do this."

"It is not the act, because I know it is necessary, though I am not happy about it. It is the possibility of finding the unknown that I am preparing myself for."

I squeeze Logan's hand as we fall into step behind the Keeper. Luckily there is no one too close when we sneak into the group of trees. Gamaliel wastes no time finding the same two trees we used to go to England.

He creates the portal and walks through, and I have to almost literally close Logan's mouth for him. As we step through, we come in the doorway of what seems like a den. There is a desk and shelf sparse with books behind us. I try to take the lead, but Logan pulls me back.

"If anyone is going to get hurt because we are here, it's me," he whispers though it's loud enough for Gamaliel to hear. "If he is here, you need to get back to the doorway and get out."

"No way am I goin-," I begin to harshly whisper before I'm interrupted.

"He is right," Gamaliel jumps in.

I huff and roll my eyes, but see no point in arguing with both of them.

We walk down the dark and empty hallway to the living room. The furniture is plain and very modern, overtly simple if you ask me. The entire home lacks a sense of invitation. It's cold, though thinking of its owner, it's really no surprise.

Logan walks over to the front windows and looks outside to ensure that Erebos' car is not parked in the driveway.

"Looks like he's gone, but he's not much of a socializer, so I wouldn't take too long. We need to do what we came to do and get the hell out of here."

"If only we knew what exactly we are here to do," I say looking around the naked living room.

We walk the house together, peering into rooms and the silence and eeriness of the house eats at me. I'm already itching to get out of here. It's not until we pass by his sliding glass door that I stop. It's dark outside so it's hard to see, but in the distance I see a fire pit with several wooden stakes and stands around it. Logan stops beside me and glares out as well.

"Well, that can't be good," he says as he grabs my hand

and pulls me along.

We walk into the strangely sterile master bedroom and begin to search around the closet and drawers careful not to leave any trace of intrusion, but come up empty. We walk back into the hallway and search the other almost empty rooms and come up with nothing.

I stand in the hallway frustrated with our results. "I can't fathom that there is nothing here, linking him to his family, magic, or his psychotic tendencies!" I lean back on the wall behind me and it gives way. Logan reaches out, catching my hand in his before I begin a backwards descent down a stairway.

He pulls me close and immediately puts me behind him. He takes his cell phone out of his pocket and turns on the light. The basement is dreary and musty, and the smell of several different herbs assault us at once.

"What the hell?" I ask as we emerge around a corner and find a large table spanning the entire wall. On it are beakers, herbs of all sorts, measuring spoons, and cups. Along the walls are shelves with old books and various bottled herbs.

As we make our way over to the table, my eye is drawn to a book at the far end. As I approach, I see that it is more of a journal than a book. "Um, guys?" They rush over to my side as I pick it up. I begin to thumb through it and find entries dating back to the 1800's. William Blackbourne writes about rituals he has created and deals he has made. A chill runs up my spine when I realize who he must have made the deals with.

I continue thumbing through until I see the words "The One." And read out loud;

If the ritual is completed during the full moon and 'The One' is sacrificed, her powers will be transferred to the Blackbournes' completing it. The Blackbournes powers will increase tenfold and the curse will be broken for the Langleys, leaving no witch or wizard powerful enough to ever stop a Blackbourne again.

The book begins to slip out of my hand, but Gamaliel takes it and continues thumbing through. I feel the rage start to boil up inside me and though Logan tries to calm me, I do not react to it.

"He doesn't just want to kill me. He wants to take my powers." I rub my face with my hands as I pace the basement. "Is this guy for real? Does he really think my powers will go to him after all the sacrifices my ancestors made?" The beakers and glass on a shelf near me take on a blue glow and I realize it's coming from my eyes.

"Babe, he isn't going to do this. We won't let him." Logan reaches out and takes my shaky hand in his. "I promise."

Gamaliel puts the book back as it was and turns to me. "I

never thought for a moment, they would have gone this far."
He rubs the short beard he's begun growing.

As we all stand there stupefied by this discovery, we hear
the front door open.

All our eyes widen and the blue glow is gone.

"We have to get out of here," Logan whispers to Gamaliel.

"I need a doorway or at least two parallel objects as tall as
us. We look around but there is no doorway, no window,
nothing."

"Does it have to be empty behind it?" Logan whispers as
he surveys the area beneath the stairs.

"What?" Gamaliel turns to him.

"Empty, does it have to be empty?" Logan asks again with
urgency as Gamaliel grabs me by the hand and drags me over.

"I have never tried it like this, but it may work."

Logan and I stand back as Gamaliel stands between two
wooden beams that help hold up the stairs, though behind
them are several boxes. He whispers his words and waves his
hand.

"I hope this works," he whispers as we hear the door at
the top of the stairs open.

I look at Logan wide eyed as light from upstairs begins to
filter in. Erebos' steps are almost as hard as my heart
pounding against my chest.

As soon as Gamaliel is through, Logan takes me and

shoves me in behind ok. I brace myself onto the Keeper, waiting for Logan, but he doesn't come through. I want to call to him, but I am afraid that Erebos will hear me. The seconds that pass seem like hours as I stand beside the trees waiting for him. After another sixty seconds or so, Logan lunges himself through and Gamaliel closes the portal.

Logan lies on the floor with his chest heaving.

"What happened?" Gamaliel extends his hand, helping Logan up.

"He stopped in the middle of the steps and looked around. I had to duck behind some boxes." He braces himself on his knees. "I thought for sure he was going to come all the way downstairs."

As I brush all the debris off Logan, he grabs my hands and studies my face. "Are you ok?" His eyebrows are pinched, but not hard and there is a hint of a frown.

I stand there staring at him and see Gamaliel waiting for my response as well out of the corner of my eye. I have no words. I just found out that Erebos intends on sacrificing me in some ritual and I can only imagine what he will do to get me there. I shake my head slowly because it's all I can do. Logan steps up and envelops me in his arms.

"Do you want some calm?" he whispers in my ear, but I shake my head again.

No, I want to deal with these insane emotions in my mind

and my heart. My biggest consolation at the moment is that my parents are far away and nobody but Logan and myself know where they are.

Gamaliel reaches out and touches my arm as Logan releases me. "I will do whatever I can and whatever you need to help you." He looks at me and then at Logan. "You will have to keep a close eye on your parents." The full moon will be here by the end of the week.

"They are safe. They went away for a few days." I don't bother telling the Keeper where they are because the less he knows about them the safer he might be.

He nods and we all begin walking back to our vehicles.

The ride home is terribly quiet, with Logan reaching over periodically and touching my cheek. He pulls in behind my jeep and we sit in the car in silence for a moment.

"You know, it's not the fighting that bothers me," I start, my eyes welling up with tears. "It's the fact that I know he isn't above hurting you, or dad, or Liz to get to me," I let them fall as I stare out the window, knowing that I can't look at him, or I would start to sob. "I can't let anything happen to you guys."

"Angel?"

I wipe my eyes and finally turn to him, reading the tone of his voice. "I'm not thinking of doing anything crazy, don't worry. The thought of that hurts more than someone wanting to kill me."

Logan takes my hand and leans over the console. "I told you, he isn't going to hurt you, or your dad, Liz, or even me. I promise you." He kisses me on the hand and then presses his lips to mine.

"Stay with me?" I ask against his lips.

He presses his forehead to mine. "Are you sure, baby? If you're not, I understand; I can just hang until you want to go to sleep, and then..."

I lift a finger to his soft lips. "I'm sure."

We make our way into the house and I immediately head to the kitchen to brew up some coffee while Logan finds something on TV for us to watch and hopefully, distract us. I return with two large mugs of coffee and stand at the entrance of the living room, watching him. He's got dark circles under his gorgeous eyes and his hair has gone from stylishly messy to messy from him dragging his hands through it all night. But he couldn't look more attractive to me. Though the TV is blaring, he's not watching it, his gaze is on the floor and he appears intensely focused. He could be anywhere with anyone and instead, he's here, with me.

He looks up and catches me staring.

"See something you like?" He raises his eyebrow and smirks.

I pucker my lips and nod slowly. "I certainly do."

He smiles and holds his arms out. I walk up, hand him his coffee and pull my legs beneath me as I snuggle up to him.

We manage to get through one TV show before the day's events start wearing on me. I feel my eyes closing and try to stop them, but despite my best efforts, sleep overtakes me. It's not until I am being carried up the stairs that I wake.

"Logan?"

"Ssh, Angel, go back to sleep, I'm just taking you to bed."

"I'm sorry I fell asleep."

"It's ok."

He gets to my bedroom and puts me down gently at the door, though I am still leaning against him.

"I have to change. I can't sleep in these jeans." I stumble over to my dresser and open a drawer, pulling out a cami and some boxer shorts. I open another drawer and pull out a pair of men's pajama pants.

"I don't know what's more disturbing, that I have those exact pants, or that you do." Logan folds his arms across his chest.

"I like guy's pajama pants better, they're just comfier," I explain as I toss the pants to him and walk by him, nudging his shoulder with mine.

By the time I emerge from the bathroom, Logan is standing in front of my dresser, folding his clothes into a neat little pile. He turns to look at me and I am stunned. He looks even better than I had pictured this morning, the pants hang low on his waist showing six of his eight pack, his chest and arms bulge tight with the muscles beneath them, it can't be more obvious that he loves his sports and working out. Geez, he could be Henry Cavill's double. I feel my knees get a little weak, but I hold my own and saunter toward him.

"Wow," Is all he needs to say for the blush to consume my body and suddenly I'm wishing I'd put the air conditioner at a lower temperature. He walks up to me slowly sliding his hands on my hips. "Are you sure you want me here? I can sleep on the sofa."

Is he kidding? You couldn't pay me to kick him out of my room right now; I don't care if the butterflies in my stomach are eating me alive!

"I'm sure."

He crawls into bed and slides over so that I can crawl right up against him. The warmth of his body against mine manages to take me away if only for moments at a time from the madness in my life. He slides his hand around my waist and laces his fingers with mine.

"This could be dangerous," he whispers into my ear and suddenly I wonder if I am leading him on. "I could get used to holding you like this and want this every night."

The weight lifts and I exhale. "You're not the only one."

CHAPTER 13

For the first night in a week I sleep through the night with no nightmares at all. I turn over slowly only to find that Logan is gone. I look at the dresser and find that his clothes are still there, but when I look at the bathroom, it's wide open with no one inside. I get up wondering where he could be, open the door, and as soon as I do, the scent of coffee and eggs makes its way up the stairs.

I lean against the entrance to the kitchen. "And you cook, too?"

Logan turns around with the wooden spoon in his hand, still shirtless and Adonis-like. "Oh, good morning, Angel. I was actually going to take this up to you," he says as he turns and continues fluffing the eggs.

I smile and walk up behind him, placing a kiss on his toned back. "You know, that's the first night in a week I haven't had nightmares."

He turns off the stove and moves the pan before turning to hug me. "Guess that means we'll have to do it again." He leans down and gives me a kiss, before lightly patting my ass and telling me to sit.

"Yes, dear!" I say as sarcastic as possible as I giggle. He brings me my coffee and a plate with perfectly scrambled eggs and toast. "I could get used to this you know."

"You're not the only one," he says so low that I almost miss it, but he glances at me to see if I did and if I caught the reference to last night.

I just smile at him and watch him eat his delicious eggs for a few moments before biting into my own.

Halfway through breakfast Logan looks up. "I have to go in a bit. I have to see my mom and take care of some things."

"Oh." I hadn't planned on what we would do today, but I took for granted that I thought he'd be here all day with me. "Alright, that's cool. Make sure you tell your mom I said hi."

"She'll like that. You going to be ok here by yourself?"

"I've stayed home alone before, Polo, and the house is still standing."

"Very funny. You know what I mean." He laughs as he

fills his mouth with his last forkful of eggs.

"I do know, and yes, I will be fine because I have no plans to go anywhere. I'll just hang here and practice my magic."

He kisses my head before he takes his stuff to the sink.

"Don't worry about the dishes. I've got it." I get up from the table, drinking my last sip of coffee.

"Are you sure?"

"Yeah." I walk up and give him a kiss. "Go check on your mom."

Logan walks out of the kitchen and about twenty minutes later, emerges again to say goodbye.

I look out the window periodically throughout the day to ensure that the gunmetal grey SUV is nowhere to be seen. Sure enough, it hasn't been which is comforting and disturbing at the same time because then I wonder if it's following Logan or trying to find my dad and Liz.

The day passes by pretty quickly since I kept myself distracted with the magic, but by the evening cabin fever sets in and as soon as Logan gets here, I beg him to take me to the rink. As if on cue, the SUV follows us there and then makes an appearance at the coffee shop afterwards.

"You alright there, babe?" The bags under Logan's eyes are worse and I wonder if he got any sleep last night. I take a sip of my chai latte and lean back on our favorite velvet couch.

He gulps down most of his chai and runs his fingers

through his hair. "Yeah, just haven't been sleeping well is all and last night's discovery didn't help that situation either."

"Well, aren't I just the thoughtful girlfriend gloating about my first full night's sleep in a week. I'm sorry." I reach over and grab his hand in mine and find that it's cold.

"Well, in your defense, it had been a week and I had a couple of good nights' sleep before then, so I guess we're even," he laughs as he pulls his hand away, wrapping them both around the steaming mug.

I reach forward and put my hand to his face. "Are you alright babe? Your hands are freezing."

"I'm fine," he sighs. "just worn, you know."

I bring my gaze down to my hands on my lap, guilt reminding me that I am part of what is wearing him out. "I'm so sorry."

His head shoots up quick. "No, no, babe. Don't. It's not you. I think it's just that finding out about my mom was the straw that broke the camel's back."

"But if it wasn't for me, you wouldn't have all these other things going on either."

"If it weren't for you, I wouldn't have these amazing feelings here." He takes my hand and puts it over his heart.

"I'll be honest, the skating helped. I can see why you feel the pull to go skating when you're stressed."

I smile, glad that I am able to bring him a quarter of the

calm that he brings to me. I shift my feet, crossing one ankle over the other and bite my lip. "So, are you staying tonight too?"

"If you want me to." He smiles over his mug at me.

Later that night, I ease into sleep with Logan's warmth enveloping me and immediately realize that I will miss this once my parents return.

"No," Logan mumbles as he tosses and turns, his chest and brow glistening with sweat as his eyes are squinted shut. "Kate...Sorry... I'm so sorry...No... don't!"

"Logan," I whisper, trying not to frighten him awake as I gently shake him. "Babe, you're having a nightmare. Wake up, Logan," I call to him softly.

Without warning, Logan bolts upright in the bed gasping for air and touching his chest.

"Logan," I call, but he is still reacting from the nightmare and doesn't hear me. "Polo!" He turns to look at me, his brow pinched and his chest heaving, still not saying a word. He looks down slowly at himself and presses his hand to his chest and exhaling hard.

"Babe," I cup his face with one hand. "It was a nightmare." I give him a minute before continuing, "You're ok."

I see his eyes water but no tears fall as he reaches out and grabs me, pulling me toward him so that I am straddling his lap. "I'm sorry." he whispers as he presses his forehead to mine.

"You didn't do anything, Polo. It was just a nightmare. Everything is ok." I pull back and look at his face as I push back the hair that is stuck to his forehead.

He presses his lips to mine with a passion he has never shown. I'm taken off guard for a moment, but quickly reciprocate, pushing hard onto his lips and opening mine to let him in. He presses me to him with an urgency that starts to worry me, but I realize that it must be the trauma of the dream and allow myself to fall into him and embrace him with the same urgency. He slowly lowers us to the bed again and neither of us is willing to let go as we envelop each other completely.

When I wake this time, Logan is still in bed and I am entangled with his legs and his arm is around me, with my head on his chest. I stay awake, listening to him breathe for more time than I can count since I didn't want to move to check my phone for the time. He starts to stir slowly and instinctively I think, pulls me closer, so I nestle my nose into his neck.

I want so bad for this to be my life, for this happiness that fills me right now to be the only thing I have to worry about. But it's not. It's nowhere close to that. I have one more day until the full moon makes its appearance and I am deathly afraid. My heart drops into my stomach and I want some of Logan's calm so bad it hurts.

"Babe?"

"Mhm?" is all I can manage.

"What's wrong?" He moves his head so that he can look in my eyes. "You're shaking."

I shake my head because I know if I open my mouth, I will cry. I think back to the last time I ever cried this much and it was when my powers first emerged and Sam labeled me a freak. I try to close myself off to it all, like I had back then, but realize that this is who I am and now I just have to face it.

"You can do this. I have faith in you, Angel, you are stronger than you know."

"But if he gets to you, or dad, or Liz...."

"He won't. I'll make sure of it." He smiles but his voice shakes.

I keep us in bed for most of the morning because I am trying to avoid confronting the day. Gamaliel and Evangeline both call and let me know that they are ready for whatever I need, reminding me how real this all is. I am surprised when Logan doesn't offer to calm me once, but then figure it's because he knows that my powers might be stronger if I am emotional.

I ask him to take me to the beach to try and enjoy some of

today before having to face the unknown tomorrow and he agrees. We pull into his driveway and make our way inside to get his bathing trunks. As Mr. Blackwell opens the door, I say hello and ask about Sabina. His face drops and says that she has decided to spend the day with a friend to take her mind off recent events.

As we are heading up the stairs, the doorbell rings again and it's Erebos. He flashes a vicious grin at us as he walks in.

"Well, if it isn't the lovebirds."

Logan's grip on my hand tightens.

Erebos looks at his nails as if he is already bored with us all. "Logan," he calls without looking up. "I need to speak with you, so be sure not to go very far."

"Sure thing, Erebos," Logan responds with a lack of emotion that prompts a quick glance from his father. He nudges me and we continue up the stairs toward his room.

"What was that about?"

"Who knows. My dad may have told him that I was showing interest in the companies now, which by the way, I found out that Erebos is forty-nine percent owner of, so unless I start my own business, I will find myself working with Erebos as well as my father." Logan shakes his head and runs his fingers through his hair. "I'm sorry, that was the other information I got from my father the other morning, so unless he sells his shares or dies, he will continue controlling my father and the businesses."

I turn him to face me as we stand in the hallway. "I'm sorry, Logan. Not to be mean, but maybe the latter will happen sooner than we know."

Logan gives a shadow of a smirk that quickly fades as Erebos emerges at the top of the stairs and stands there, waiting for us to acknowledge his presence.

"I'll go talk to him. Who knows, maybe I can find out some of his plans for tomorrow," Logan whispers to me as he opens the door to his room. "Wait here for me."

He gives me a quick kiss on the cheek and makes his way down the hall.

As soon as I get into the room, I begin to wonder where they could have gone since I heard them descending the stairs. My attention is quickly turned to the bookshelf that leads downstairs. I make my way over and pull out The Secret Garden just as Logan had done the other day, push it down and then back in again. The locks give way and the door springs open. I make my way quietly down the stairs, using my phone to light the way. When I reach the bottom, I am tempted to open the latch and go into the den to find them, but I hear voices and wait, with my hand on the latch.

"What do you want, Erebos?" Logan sounds very firm, much steadier than he had earlier this morning.

"I must say that I was very surprised to receive your call

yesterday." Erebos's voice is sly and low, but there was no mistaking what he said.

Why would Logan call him?

"Did you consider my proposal?" Logan responds coldly.

"Are you sure you can do it?" I hear Erebos walking around the room. "You seem very attached to her."

"If it will help my mother. I will do it." Logan responds firmly.

What the hell are they talking about?

"You realize what that will entail, correct?" Erebos stops pacing. "You will have to be the one to lure her in, you will have to be the one to sacrifice her so that your healing powers become stronger and you can try to help your mother, and save our family name of course."

"Of course," Logan agrees.

No. My eyes fill with silent tears that fall almost immediately.

"She trusts me," he continues, "and I know where her parents are, it will be easy to bring her to us."

"Again, you are sure?" Erebos walks around some more and I wonder if he has walked over to Logan. "Love does things to people Logan, it tests their loyalty."

"But blood comes before love." he finishes firmly.

I put my hand to my mouth to keep from sobbing and hold on tight to the latch to keep my knees from buckling beneath me.

He can't... why would he... his mom...

Incoherent thoughts drift in and out of my head at the speed of a train and I can't wrap my head around what I have just heard.

"Babe?" I hear Logan's voice drifting down from his room. "Shit!" I hear him step into the secret passage and I lunge myself to the door that leads outside. "Katelyn!"

I run across his yard, jumping over small hedges and tripping over the brick edging of a flower bed, scraping my knee. I slam into the black iron gates hard and my hands burn as I grab onto it, trying to shake it free.

I look back to find Logan gaining ground on me, and see the button to open the gate. I quickly run over and press it wishing the enormous gates would open faster. I start squeezing through them just as Logan approaches and grabs my hand.

"Dammit, Kate! Where are you going?" Logan yells, trying to pull me back, but I yank his arm against the gates, hurting him and forcing him to lighten his grip enough for me to wriggle out.

"Away from you!" I yell, before I sprint down the street and I see him retreat into his house, likely to get his truck keys.

I duck behind a shrub two blocks up from his house as he drives past me. My phone buzzes off the hook in my pocket and I decline his calls. As soon as he turns I emerge and continue running up the block, grateful that I didn't have my flip flops on. I make it to the yacht club and finally pull out my phone to call a cab. I have over a dozen missed calls and texts telling me that I don't understand.

I sit on the sidewalk at the corner of the yacht club until the cab pulls up. As soon as I stand it occurs to me that I need to text my parents, but what exactly do I tell them?

Hi, mom and dad, if you get a call or visit from Logan, just ignore him because he has lost his mind and thinks that if he sacrifices me he will gain power to heal his mom. No biggie.

The cab driver looks back a couple of times and on the third offers a tissue since I can't seem to stop crying. With a Puerto Rican accent, he tells me that I am too pretty and young to be crying so much. When he pulls up to my house, Logan is sitting on my porch. The cab driver must have noticed my hesitation since he offers to keep going and take me somewhere else, free of charge. I decline with a smile and step out, handing him his money. As soon as I step onto my walkway and close the gate behind me, Logan stands and begins walking toward me. His eyes are red and his long lashes are wet. His chest is heaving and he opens his mouth, but I raise my hand, asking him to stop.

I open my mouth, but instead tears fall and I choke on the words I am going to say. "I'll do whatever you want, just don't hurt my dad or Liz."

"Angel, ple-"

"Don't!" I yell and the tears come harder. "Don't call me that!" I choke out between sobs. I walk around him and up to my porch and he follows me, but stops at the steps. Wind whips around us and strips nearby branches of their leaves.

"I just," he tries, but I turn to unlock my door. "I'm trying to do the right thing here."

I chuckle through the sobs. "The right thing," I say lowly. "There is no right thing now is there?" I raise my hands and slam them down onto my thighs. "I should have seen it! At least with you having all the power, you can save your mom and maybe stop Erebos from controlling your dad the way he does! Should you want to stop there."

"That's what you see?" Logan shouts and his eyes well up with tears.

"No," I say as calmly as I can, wiping the tears from my cheeks. "That's what I heard. From your mouth." I bite my lip, stopping more tears from falling. "So go ahead and kill me, just leave my dad and Liz out of this. I'll come quietly, after all, it can't hurt more than it does right now."

I walk in and slam the door behind me before dropping to my knees. I think of what I would do if I had the chance to stop my dad from suffering, but I can't. It's just not something I can picture because the pain in my chest won't allow it.

I hear his tires screech in the street as he makes his way out for what is almost the last time. I spend the rest of the day hating myself for letting him in, for falling for him, and most of all for agreeing to check Erebos' house, even though it might have given a solution to healing his mom. My thoughts return to last night when he had the nightmare and I realize that he was struggling with what he was doing to me. That must be why he was apologizing to me. My heart sinks further as I picture the entire night over and over in my mind.

As it gets later, I text my dad and ask what time he will be back tomorrow and he says it should be around five or six. I breathe a sigh of relief and decide to go to Logan before then, because I will not be able to bear saying goodbye to them.

I spend almost the entire night awake, falling asleep every once in a while for fifteen or twenty minutes but never any more than that. When I decide I can no longer stare at my ceiling, I get up and take a shower. I slip into my jeans, my black tank top, and my sneakers. *What do you wear to be sacrificed, anyway?* I pull my hair into a ponytail and look at myself in the mirror. *I don't have anyone to impress, so this will have to do.* The bags under my eyes have almost overtaken my face. I look years older than I did before the school year was over. My chest heaves and I look at my room for the last time.

I walk over to the small desk in the corner of my room and take the pictures of my dad and Liz and of my mom out of their frames. My chin shakes, but I keep the tears in, or I've run out, I'm not sure anymore.

I'm so numb, I feel like I am barely in control of my own movements. The need for nourishment eludes me, though nausea continues to plague me.

I look at my phone and see that it's noon. I silently wonder what will become of me, what will Logan tell my parents? Will he tell them I'm missing? Will he say we had an accident? Every scenario I think of turns my stomach even more. I walk around my home one more time and stand at my parent's bedroom for at least thirty minutes.

Well, no point in delaying the inevitable. At two o clock, I jump in my jeep and drive to Logan's house, though I do not remember how I got there since my mind wandered the whole time. I pull up to his house and sit in my car for another twenty minutes. I finally step out of the car and make my way to the door.

Sabina answers it and I am bombarded by feelings of hate, sorrow and anguish. I know it's not her fault, but I can't help but blame her at least a little. Judging by the smile on her face, she has no idea what her son is up to, so I play along.

"Hello, Katelyn! It is so great to see you." She takes me into a hug and releases me, looking around the room to ensure that no one hears what she is about to say. "I was starting to think that something happened between you and Logan because he's been so sad and distant the past couple of days."

I take a ragged breath. "Nothing we can't work through, Sabina. Is he home?"

"Yes, dear, he is upstairs. I'm going to run to the mall for a bit and do some retail therapy." She raises an eyebrow and smirks. "Hubby's orders. He thinks it will make me feel better." She shrugs her shoulders. "It couldn't hurt," she giggles slightly, takes her purse off the coatrack and heads out the door.

My feet are heavy with each step I take and though part of me wants to get it over with, the other part wants to turn and go home.

I knock on Logan's door before opening it and find him sitting on the chair on his balcony.

"You're early."

I open my mouth to speak, but the sight of him renders me speechless. Part of me still cannot believe that he is going to go through with this. "I didn't want to be home when dad and Liz got there."

"I figured as much,." he says solemnly, still not looking at me.

I walk out to the balcony and breathe in the sea air mixed with the smell of all the flowers from the garden. Though I try to let it soothe me, it doesn't work. I look at Logan's hand and want to take it so bad and beg him not to do this, but I don't.

Instead, I sit down beside him. I see his fingers twitch but he doesn't move.

"Is... Is it going to hurt?"

"I will try to make it painless." His voice shakes ever so slightly as he keeps his attention on the distant sea.

I take some deep breaths and they are each ragged. I look at him out of the corner of my eye and I see him looking at me, his eyes are sad and red and I know that part of him is dying over this decision, but still, I say nothing.

"Have you contacted Gamaliel?" he asks hesitantly.

"No. He won't understand and doesn't need to know."

We sit in silence for a long time, with me forcing the wind to swirl around us, bringing the aroma of the flowers up to us every once in a while offering what little comfort it can. After an hour he checks his watch, gets up and walks into his room. He almost staggers over to the sofa and leans on it, turning pale and I think that he is about to puke all over it.

"Logan," I whisper, torn between wanting to comfort him and punch him in the gut so he feels some pain at my hands.

Just then, my phone vibrates in my pocket. I pull it out to find a message from my dad.

Tell Logan thanks, we appreciate him sending his boat to pick us up. Can't wait to see you guys later tonight.

I run to his balcony and look out to the pier to see that his boat is gone.

When I turn around, Logan is leaning against his sofa, facing me. I feel a rage build inside me and for the first time ever, I ball up my hands to keep the magic from bursting out and possibly hurting myself as well. I stomp over to him as a tear rolls down my face and he doesn't move, not until my knuckles crunch against his jaw, sending him over the sofa, breaking the coffee table and landing against the other sofa.

"What are you doing?!" I yell as I watch him rub his chin and arch his back. "I told you I would be here! I told you, you could do whatever you wanted, just to leave them out of this."

He takes a deep breath and pushes himself off the floor, his gaze only resting on me for a moment. I want to read his emotions, but I can't. He looks like he is fighting over himself between anger and hate, and rage and even sadness. "I had to be sure you weren't going to back out." He moves his jaw back and forth as he walks to the shelf that leads to the secret passage. "You coming?" he calls over his shoulder at me.

I want to scream. I want to push him down the stairs and punch him, punch him until he hurts as bad as I do. I want to hit him in the heart so it will break into a million pieces like mine. But I don't. I walk silently to the passage while tears roll down my face. I follow him out into the garden and though the sun warms my face, I am nothing but cold inside.

Logan opens his mouth like he is going to say something but doesn't and I can't decide if I want him to or not. The wind whips through my hair as if it's trying to comfort me, but I barely acknowledge it. We walk to his dock and Erebos is waiting for us. I have an overwhelming urge to knock him off and drown him in the water, but with my parents on Logan's boat I find myself keeping my hands at my sides. We walk to the very end and I begin to see his boat appear in the distance.

My phone vibrates again and it's my dad.

Hey, Katie-Kat! I'm in the bridge and can see you with the binoculars. I can't wait to get there. I got you and Logan something from Martha's Vineyard.

I choke back my tears in case he is still watching and try to keep a smile on my face. As the boat comes closer, I see my dad and Liz standing at the top and waving before disappearing moments later below deck.

"Just..." I start, my voice is low so that only Logan can hear me, "Just please don't..."

My voice trails off as I hear an explosion and when I turn

my attention to the ocean, the entire ship is engulfed in flames.

"Nooooo!" I scream as I reach out my hands and collapse to my knees. "What have you done?!" I feel my insides heave, but I have nothing to spew so I stare off the water to the ball of flames that has incinerated my parents. When I look down at my reflection in the water, my eyes are glowing blue and my hands are trembling. The water around us begins to roil, splashing so hard against the posts below they begin to crack. I lunge at Logan, knocking him off his feet and knocking his head onto the dock.

Out of the corner of my eye, I see Erebos pull something from his coat pocket. He takes the lid off and a needle sparkles in the remaining sunlight.

"Now, now, let's not waste that precious power just yet." He throws himself onto me and plunges the needle into my neck.

Just as the darkness begins to envelop me, I collapse onto Logan, completely blinded and hearing only three words, "I'm sorry, Angel."

CHAPTER 14

When I wake I am tied to a makeshift crucifix, only I'm on my knees and my ankles are chained to the concrete behind me. Leather straps hold my arms out to either side. The first thing I think of when I open my eyes is the sight of the burning boat that my parents had been in.

I feel the same sensation to throw up, but there is nothing in my stomach, so I end up heaving once and sobbing until I see Logan and Erebos emerge from Erebos' home, followed by two older gentlemen all dressed in black with guns strapped to their hips. I figure that those must have been the two in the gunmetal grey SUV. I completely ignore the two goons and run my gaze briefly over Erebos, locking my sights on Logan.

As they approach, one of the goons circles me, running his finger along my neck and pushing my hair to my back.

"You sure we can't have a little fun with her before we sacrifice her? Seems kind of a waste if you ask me."

Logan lunges forward grabbing him by the shirt and speaking through gritted teeth, "You touch her again, and I'll sacrifice you…Got it?"

The goon puts up both his hands and backs up slowly.

Logan spares a glance at me, but I shift my gaze, unable to accept even that moment of kindness.

Erebos kneels in front of me and picks up my chin with two fingers. "You should be proud that you will be contributing your magic to Logan. With his youth and drive, he will be able to do great things for our family…" He smacks his lips together. "Oh, and he will have a piece of you with him the whole time."

I shake my head out of his hand and spit in his direction. "Go to hell."

Erebos gives a wicked laugh. "Perhaps one day, but not just yet." He stands, turning his attention to Logan. "Don't take too long with your goodbyes my great nephew, we have preparations to make," Erebos warns Logan, pointing a finger at him.

Logan waits until Erebos is halfway to his home before

kneeling in front of me. I can't bring myself to look at him, so I let my head hang and stare at the ground that I slowly saturate with my tears. He reaches out and grazes his fingers along my head and down to my neck. I flinch, yanking on the leather straps and even the chains at my ankles.

"I begged you. I begged you to leave them out of it." I sniff as more tears fall and I shake my head. "They didn't have to die. Especially, not because of me." I watch my tears disturb the dust beneath me.

Logan runs his hands along my arms and over the leather cuffs and I don't know if he is trying to be close to me, or make sure that I am tied down, but I'm not sure I care. He presses his head to mine. "I'm sorry. It wasn't supposed to be this way," he whispers onto my cheek, forcing more tears, but this time I lift my head to look into his eyes. Those eyes, which are now a dark blue, with all light having left them.

"No, I am sorry," I say lowly as I feel the tingle taking over my body and see the reflection of the glow of my eyes in his. His face flickers, his eyes widen and he stands slowly backing away. I feel the pulse in my hands, but the restraints are too tight.

I think about calling Gamaliel, but I am afraid of causing someone else to lose his life on my account, so I remove all thoughts of him from my mind, barring him from finding me.

Erebos makes his way back and throws more logs on the

fire to my right, causing embers to fly out and fry bits of my flesh, but I don't react. He pulls two vials from his pocket and empties them into the fire, changing the color of the flames to blue the first time and the second, the entire pit glowed green. He chants some words in a language I have never heard and never care to again as he waves his hands over the fire, causing the smoke to carry to him as he inhales. He calls Logan over so that he can do the same, but leaves Logan there while he saunters his way over to me.

"Oooh," he clicks his tongue once. "Well, Logan, you seem to have enraged our fair little maiden here. Look at her." He stands back admiring me. "Come, nephew, come see." He waves Logan over to stand beside him and he puts his arm around Logan's shoulder. "Do you know why her eyes glow, when that has not happened to any witch in history?"

Logan does not respond, but only shakes his head.

"It is the centuries of power she contains. It is the power you will have, my boy, once tonight is over."

"Not if I can stop him." I say arrogantly.

"What will you do little witch?" Erebos lunges at me grabbing my face in his hands.

I smirk at him, "First, I will kill you, then I will stop him."

"Stop him?" Erebos releases my face violently and begins to chuckle loudly. "*Not*, kill him?" He puts his hand over his chest. "Oh bleeding heart, you love him." He laughs harder.

Logan's eyes widen, but he doesn't move or say anything.

"Well, dear girl, I will tell you something then," he puts his lips next to my ear. "I killed your parents. Logan just wanted to use them as insurance, but I made sure that the boat never made it back to port."

He pulls his face back and looks me in the eyes. "So let that console you while you die at his hands." He turns to Logan. "It's time."

I am left there for what I estimate to be about thirty minutes in which time the goons run back and forth from the house, bringing candles, potions, and the journal. Logan does little except supervise and on occasion glance at me, though I keep my emotion to myself.

"Logan, be sure her restraints are tight. We have no idea how strong she can be when her powers maximize.

Logan walks over to me, trying not to look me in the eyes as he pulls on the restraints and re-does the buckles in the back. He steps over to my left with his hands behind his back as Erebos begins chanting something again in that foreign language I have never heard. He crashes a beaker full of red liquid onto the logs on the fire, causing the fire to blaze up, the heat causing me to turn my head, and I begin to perspire.

I try to look back, but the blaze doesn't come back down. Erebos walks over to the fire inserting a dagger into the flames until it begins to scorch his hand. He begins to make his way to me, and out of the corner of my eye, I see Evangeline and Gamaliel run out from a nearby set of trees, attacking the two goons who sit on the other end of the pit. The two goons pull their guns and shoot them, knocking them down, but they are back up within seconds and chasing them.

"Stop them!" Erebos yells, the dagger burning him. "Do not let them stop us!"

I begin to see flashes of grey and white lights as the guns go off again.

Erebos walks toward me with the dagger pointed at me, and Logan pulls a knife from his waist, turning and slicing one of the leather cuffs that are holding me down.

As soon as my arm is free, I point it at Erebos who is now no more than one foot away from me. A flash of blue and white appear and I knock him into the air landing him easily five feet away from me. I feel the surge of energy and when I pull on the chains I realize they are already undone and that Logan must have done that when Erebos told him to check my restraints. I look at Logan and only see my parents on the burning boat and let my rage loose on him as well, knocking him down and away from me. I reach over to undo my other strap, when out of the corner of my eye I see Erebos running toward me. The latch gets stuck and I fire at him with all I have but he jumps out of the way.

The fire nearby blazes and I pull from it, trying to engulf

him in flames, but he puts them out and I realize that he must have elemental powers as well. He comes at me, wrapping both his hands around my neck, I flail my free hand, trying to claw at his face, and though I scratch him and blood runs down his cheek, I cannot stop him. He starts chanting again and I realize that I will have to try something else. I stare at him and picture myself going into his mind. I have to push hard and though my mind is hurting and out of the corner of my eye, I see Gamaliel holding Evangeline back, I continue forward, remembering that Keepers can only do so much, the rest is on me.

I stumble into the darkness that is Erebos' mind and begin to see flashes of rituals, beatings at the hands of those loyal to the cause, and introduction to this darkness by his father. I try to inflict pain just by thought and he closes his eyes, his words slurring, but I am running out of air and cannot keep this up. He releases my neck and takes a step back, finishing his chant and dropping the blade down.

Just as the blade catches the reflection of the fire next to me, Logan lunges on top of me.

"Aaaaaah!" I hear Logan right in my ear.

"Logan!" I scream as his body becomes heavier on me and he slowly glides off onto the ground with a dagger protruding from his back.

"No!" Erebos screams. "You fool!" He staggers back. "I

should have known you would be weak! I should have known you couldn't do this!"

He yanks the dagger from Logan's back and I finally manage to free my other hand. I take all the energy inside me and lift my hands in his direction, just as the dagger comes down on me again, but he only manages to scratch my chest as he is blown back and suspended in air.

"You and your family's evil will die here!" I scream at him, though it is not my voice. It is a voice I heard only once before in my head. Abigail.

I release all the energy I have left and Erebos is thrown hard against one of the pillars surrounding the fire pit, splintering the thick wood and falling lifeless to the ground.

I drop to my knees and crawl over to Logan. I see Gamaliel finally release Evangeline as he goes over to Erebos, probably to ensure he is dead. Evangeline runs to me, taking me in her arms.

"Oh my precious girl. My Katelyn!" She holds me to her as she runs her hands down my head and back. "You did it. You've released us from the curse and stopped the Blackbournes."

At the sound of the name, I ease out of her grip and look at her for a moment, before turning to Logan. I crawl over to him and hesitate, as I see Evangeline go around him and kneel immediately trying to check him for a pulse. She looks at me and puts her hands over where the dagger was plunged.

I feel the hot tears streaming down my face as I watch his still body, waiting for a reaction. Evangeline's eyes are closed and her hands are trembling, beneath them the wound seems to slowly stop gushing blood. "You can heal?"

Evangeline drops from her knees onto the ground like she has been drained of all her energy. "Only a little, his body will have to do the rest. Perhaps his own gift of healing will be enough."

Gamaliel walks up to us and nods his head slowly. "It is balanced once again." His eyes drop quickly to Logan.

I crawl around to his other side and Evangeline moves to give me room. I lie next to him on the ground, still feeling the heat of the nearby fire. "Please, Logan." I wipe my eyes. "Don't do this." My chin quivers as I swallow the lump in my throat and continue, "we will still find a way to help your mom, but you have to stay with me." I grab his hand and put it on my face as Gamaliel examines the wound on his back. I fight with myself over feelings of anger and sadness.

Gamaliel looks at me with his brows furrowed. "We have to get out of here."

"What's going to happen to us? What about when someone finds out who did this?"

Evangeline slides a hand under me pushing me up. "There are others who will ensure this is 'balanced'. But we have to go now."

I stand to my feet, my eyes still on Logan. "What about Logan?"

Gamaliel, lifts him up by an arm and throws his limp body over his own shoulders. "Now!" He yells as he begins to make his way to the nearby forest from which they had first emerged. I run behind him with Evangeline at my side. As soon as he chooses the parallel path, he creates a portal and we are in his living room where I was the first time I was attacked.

"Shouldn't we be in a hospital?" I ask loudly as the Keeper lowers Logan onto his sofa.

"No," Gamaliel says firmly as Evangeline runs to another room and emerges only moments later with a first aid kit.

"Clean him. I will be right back."

Gamaliel disappears into the kitchen and I help Evangeline soak cotton balls with peroxide, cleaning up the wound. I see Logan's fingers twitch a couple of times, but otherwise he gives no reaction. As we are cleaning up, Gamaliel walks into the room with a teacup filled with a liquid whose steam stops short of bubbling over the cup instead of going up into the air around it. He searches the first aid kit and finds a syringe. He takes the lid off with his teeth and spits it onto the floor.

The Keeper inserts the needle into the hot liquid and pulls

some out into the syringe. He holds it carefully over the open wound, allowing only a few drops to fall in, and I see pieces of tissue and flesh begin to merge. He takes out some butterfly strips, to assist in closing the wound from the outside, puts a bandage over it and some first aid tape to hold it in place.

"Help me," he tells Evangeline and she moves to stand above Logan's head to support him as they turn him over and lay him partially on his back, careful to not put pressure on the wound.

Evangeline brings her hands down over his mouth and opens it. Logan doesn't move, does not protest; he is so still I would have mistaken him for dead.

Gamaliel shakes his head. "That will take too long." He lifts Logan's shirt revealing his severely bruised abdomen. "The damage she caused is too much. It has to be direct." He raises his hand and brings it down hard on Logan's stomach, driving the needle down all the way in. He injects more liquid into Logan's body than he had into the wound as he pulls the needle free, he puts Logan's shirt back down and sighs, sitting on the coffee table.

"Now, we wait."

I gasp at the revelation that the 'she' that Gamaliel is talking about is me. "Me."

"What dear?" Evangeline furrows her brow as she watches my face and walks over to a nearby seat, plopping herself down.

"Me. I'm the one who did that to him." My gaze shifts from each Keeper to Logan. "I was mad that he didn't leave my parents out of it, like I asked. They would have never died if it had not been for him."

Gamaliel and Evangeline look at each other and suddenly I see Mr. Wentworth again. That gaze that tells me that he wants to say something to me, but can't.

"You are welcome to stay and see if Logan makes it through the night." The keeper picks up the first aid kit, the tea cup, and the syringe pieces and makes his way out of the living room.

"What do you mean if? The stuff you gave him is supposed to heal him, right?" I beg as I make my way to sit on the floor next to Logan.

"It's not a miracle, Katelyn. It will help, but the rest is out of our hands." He turns the corner and is gone.

I look at Logan and am torn between wanting him to live because he saved me from Erebos and not wanting him to live because of what he did to my parents. I realize that I have never wished death on anyone and I'm not sure I even want it now.

I lift myself onto the edge of the sofa and look at Logan's face. I wipe the dirt away and move the tendrils of hair that have stuck to his forehead, cursing myself for feeling the way

I do. I take out my phone and read my dad's last texts to me and flip through all the saved pictures I have.

I take a pillow from the end of the sofa and lower myself onto it while my eyelids become heavier and heavier.

When I wake in the morning it's to Logan's voice.

"No..." I hear him shift on the sofa and then groan when he leans on his wound, forcing him the other way. "Angel... No!" he screams as he jolts up on the sofa and immediately reaches for his abdomen and hisses at the pain.

I get up slowly and ease myself onto the coffee table, watching him. I want to comfort him, but the rage that is still fueled inside me keeps me from him.

I hear Gamaliel and Evangeline come into the room, likely in response to Logan's scream.

Logan turns his head and his gaze is immediately on me, though it is only for a moment since Gamaliel steps between us.

"Lay back, Logan." He forces Logan back and hovers his hands over his abdomen. "I do not sense any permanent damage or bleeding. How is your shoulder?"

"Hurts," is all he says as he tries to look around the Keeper at me.

"That may last for a while I am afraid." Gamaliel looks at me and then back at Logan and shakes his head. He stands again and glances over at Evangeline, giving a ghost of a smile. "I will make us some coffee."

Logan throws his legs over and sits himself up, groaning as he leans forward.

I extend my hand, but retract it immediately. "Th.. Thank you for saving me."

"I told you, Angel. Oh." He clutches his abdomen again and guilt shoots through me. "I wasn't going to let anything happen to you." He stands, though he is barely able. "You made the same promise about my parents."

"I did." He drops his gaze to his feet as he chews on his lip and sighs as he walks forward slowly. "Gamaliel."

The keeper enters the room "I have to speak with Kate if you please."

Gamaliel presses his lips together and nods before nudging his head in the direction of the doorway.

I see Gamaliel hug Logan and realize it is likely the first and maybe the last time I will see that much emotion from the Keeper.

"Thank you," Logan says lowly to him.

I follow Logan to the door, though I have little desire to do so, I feel as if we are still imposing on Gamaliel.

Evangeline emerges from the kitchen and looks at me, her eyes are sad and her smile is fallen. She walks up and takes me in her arms. "Please don't forget the promise you made me."

"I won't forget," I whisper onto her shoulder.

CHAPTER 15

Logan opens the door and begins to step through and I follow behind, not knowing where we are going, and honestly not caring at the moment. What I really want to do is be alone with the million thoughts in my head now that I know he has lived through the wounds.

As soon as my feet hit the ground I see the familiar wooden floors beneath my dirty sneakers. I lift my head and my stomach turns as we have walked into the doorway of my kitchen. I look around at the cabinet, appliances, and tables that all hold memories I never thought I would live to remember, though now the memories taste bittersweet.

Logan collapses into a seat at the breakfast table, causing

it to scrape against the floor. Almost immediately, I hear footsteps pounding down the stairs.

"Katie-Kat!?" My father's voice echoes into the room and my eyes fill with tears. "Lynnie!" I hear Liz running right behind him.

I stand stunned as my dad barrels into the kitchen without stopping and scoops me up in his arms and I sob onto his shoulder. Liz crashes into us, wrapping her arms around us both.

"How are you... But I saw you…" I manage to choke out as my dad puts me down and wipes the tears on my face.

"Logan," my dad says very matter of fact.

My gaze shifts to Logan who is looking on with a pained smile on his face.

"I.. I don't understand." I shake my head, "I saw you on the boat… I saw it blow up." I wipe my face with the back of my hand.

"What you didn't see was your boyfriend calling me and showing up at Martha's Vineyard the day after you two discovered what Erebos was doing." My dad folds his arms across his chest proudly as he glances at Logan. "It was quite a surprise."

"But, you didn't say… You told me…" I was starting to get mad at myself for not being able to complete a damn sentence.

"When I saw what Erebos wanted to do, I knew that he would not hesitate to go after Rick and Liz. I stayed up all night trying to come up with a plan." Logan pushes himself onto his feet. "The next morning, I called your dad as soon as I left you." My dad shoots a glare at me and I ignore it, though I feel a blush creep up. "I also called Erebos. I told him that I needed to speak to him. I knew it would take two hours to get to your parents by boat so I went straight home, grabbed the boat and met them at the house they were staying at. I know you didn't want to tell them about your powers just yet, Angel, but it was the only way."

"He even showed us his powers, so we can see that you weren't alone," Liz interjects, smiling sweetly and wiping the tears from her face.

"I told them about Erebos, about you and I, and even about Gamaliel who I called on the way to see your parents. I realized that the only way Erebos would keep some sort of distance from you, is if I was helping him. I used my mother's illness as an excuse for wanting to get involved with him and he bought it. I never thought you would hear us talking, but it worked out for the better, because it was hard enough looking at you, knowing what I was doing and was going to do."

"But the boat? That still doesn't explain what I saw."

"Erebos wasn't going to leave your parents out of it; I

know because he mentioned that he needed to get you to use your maximum powers that night so that it would be transferred to him. How else, but to make you suffer that much? So I came up with the idea of offering to pick them up on the boat. Knowing he wouldn't wait for them to arrive, I asked Gamaliel to be the one picking them up."

I brought my hand to my mouth. "He portaled them out before Erebos had a chance to kill them," I finish for him, the entire plan playing out in my head, as anger wins over as the current emotion of choice. "Dammit, Logan, I could have killed you, how did you know I wouldn't kill you?" I bury my face in my hands, tears streaming down as I picture my attack on him.

"I didn't. But I told you I wouldn't let anything happen to you, your dad, or Liz." He glances at each of them and nods at my dad.

Liz pouts her lip and walks over to Logan, putting her arms around him until he hisses and she let go. "Oh my gosh, Logan, are you hurt?" She sees the bandage through his torn shirt and tells him to sit. "I'll get you something for the pain, sweetie." She rushes out of the room and I hear her run up the stairs.

Logan lowers himself onto the chair as pain etches itself across every inch of his face.

"I punched you!" I put my hands up to my mouth and out

of the corner of my eye I see my dad's eyes widen as he cocks his head. "That's why you looked like you were going to be sick. You knew what it would do to me and you let me hurt you. You let me take out my pain on you." I walk to him slowly as tears fall again and I kneel in front of him, reaching my hand to his abdomen. "I hurt you at Erebos'. I almost killed you and you still threw yourself in front of his knife for me."

Liz returns with the pills but leaves them on the table with a glass of water as she and my dad leave us alone in the kitchen.

"But you didn't kill me. You had a few chances and you didn't do it." Logan's lips curl into a smile. "You never even told me you hated me. Which, by the way, did make that a bit harder," he lets out a short chuckle.

"I wanted to hurt you. I wanted you to feel my pain," I say as I drag a chair to me and sit on it so that my knees are touching the edge of his seat and I am as close to him as I can get.

"I was hurting. I was dying inside, doing that to you, but I knew that if you thought I turned on you, if you thought your parents were dead, you would have enough rage to kill Erebos when I helped you get free." Logan lifts a hand to my cheek. "My heart broke that day on your porch. I wanted to let you in on it, but I needed you to believe it, so that Erebos would believe it too. Especially, when you said you would do it to help my mom." He shakes his head. "As awesome as it would be to do more, what I told you before is true … The healing we can do, can't cure that."

"Why did you do it, Logan?" I press my face into his palm. "You risked your life. You risked me taking your life to protect my family and I."

"Isn't it obvious, Angel?" He gives another smile through the hurt. "I love you."

I ease myself onto his lap, careful not to hurt him and press my lips to his. Despite his bruising, he pulls me tight and I hear him groan against my lips before he releases me a bit. I press my forehead against his, looking into his eyes which are almost back to their radiant blue. "I love you too, Polo." I breathe onto his lips with a smile. "The whole time, even when I was mad, even when my heart was broken, I loved you with every piece of it."

EPILOGUE

I run down the stairs and open the door to find two beautiful pools of blue staring back at me. Logan leans down and scoops me up, dropping snow on the floor as he places his lips on mine.

"Hey, Harvard girl," he says onto my lips just before he lets me go so I can reach for my boots by the door.

"Well, not yet, my first day isn't for another couple of weeks. But it was nice to hear that they got the transcripts from the University of Connecticut."

I slide my boots on and glide into the new black leather coat that Logan gave me for Christmas before grabbing my purse shuffling through the snow to his car.

As soon as we get in the car, Logan begins rotating his arm at the shoulder.

"Are you alright?" I reach over, rubbing lightly over the scar on his shoulder blade.

"Yeah, stupid cold is making it act up." He turns his head to me and smiles, wiggling his eyebrows. "Are you ready?"

"Yes!" I jump up and down in my seat like a child, clutching my purse hard.

For the most part, the ride is pretty quiet with the exception of talks of the new commercial real estate office and investment firms that Logan and his dad are opening. I ask about his mom and he smiles.

"She's doing much better. She's on a medication that has been proven to even reverse some of the effects."

I reach over and grab his hand in mine. "That is great news!"

"And how's everything with your dad?"

Logan lets out a chuckle. "Well, I should start by telling you that he has totally attributed my new change in attitude about the business and my relationship with him to you."

"Well, I am kinda great," I snort.

He glances at me out of the corner of his eye and chuckles. "Yes, yes, you are. It's great, though to see how different" he responds now that Erebos doesn't have control over him and it's a relief to finally know that he never used his powers the way Erebos did to control anyone." He shrugs his shoulder and smirks while still looking out the windshield. "I don't know, It's almost made me want to work harder with him, knowing that everything he's built, he's done on his own, you know?"

"I know." I place a proud kiss on the back of his hand and bring it back down to my lap. "I'm proud of you, babe."

It's not long before we begin our drive along the cobblestone streets of the famous Beacon Hill in Boston. No matter how many times we have visited, the gas lamps and beautiful three story brick homes always take me back to a time where I picture the horses and carriages and women in beautiful gowns strolling beneath the dim street lights.

"I can't imagine a place that is more you." he says as he shuts off the SUV and steps out.

I smile as he gets out of the car and walks around to open my door.

We turn up the brick walkway and the eight or so black steps that lead to the tucked away front door. We knock on the door and a middle aged woman with blonde hair and bright red lipstick opens.

"Mr. Blackwell, Ms. Miller, how are you doing this evening?"

"Fine, Daria, thank you," Logan answers as we walk across the threshold.

We follow her into the home, passing the beautiful open staircase on the left next to the small office and past the old world decorated living room with the oversized sofa tables and entertainment center. We enter the breakfast room which leads to the enormous open kitchen with dark cabinets and an island and take a seat at the oak breakfast table.

Daria pushes a stack of papers toward us. "I've marked all the areas I need you both to sign."

We take the pages and two fountain pens on top and Logan begins to speed read through every page, stopping only when we have to jot down our names or signatures.

As Logan reads through the contract, I see Daria glancing several times at the antique style diamond ring on my left hand. I catch her eye one time and smile, prompting her to ask a question that had been apparently sitting on the tip of her tongue.

"So how long have you two been engaged?" She leans on the table eagerly.

I glance at Logan who looks up from the papers for a moment to smile at us both.

"Two weeks, he proposed on Christmas morning during Christmas breakfast in front of both our families," I answer with a smile so wide, my cheeks start to hurt and I'm pretty sure that's a blush I feel.

"That is so sweet," Daria says as she pouts a lip at us.

"Well, family is important to us," Logan says, looking up just long enough to give me a wink.

Once we are done, we hand the stack of papers back to Daria and she hands us the key to our new home.

No sooner does Logan close the door behind her than he turns to look at me.

"Well, soon-to-be Mrs. Blackwell, what do you think?"

"I think the same thing as last time. It's enormous, too expensive, and you shouldn't have. But you didn't listen then, Polo, so no point in dwelling on that." I roll my eyes exaggeratingly before smiling and throwing my arms around his neck and laughing. "I think that anywhere with you is home." I press my lips against his. "And I absolutely love it."

He turns me around, still keeping his arms around me and we both look around our home and sigh.

"I want to show you something that I have managed to keep Daria from telling you about," he whispers in my ear before lightly kissing my lobe.

"What's that?" I turn, putting my hands on my hips.

He gives me a mischievous smile. "Come along." Logan takes my hand, leads me to the third floor, and takes me past our den which is wall to wall and floor to ceiling bookshelves, broken only by a marble fireplace in the center of the far wall that we have surrounded with high back chairs and small tables for us to sit and read. I smile quickly as I catch sight of the red velvet loveseat that used to sit in the coffee shop. It took some sweet talking and the promise of two other similar pieces, but Logan managed to coerce the owners into selling it.

"You wanted to show me the linen closet?" I raise a brow as I follow Logan to the end of the hallway and he takes hold of a doorknob.

"Not really." Logan opens the door and I see a set of stairs.

"You said this was just another linen closet!"

"Well, yeah, how else would I keep you from looking around? I figured if you've seen one linen closet, you've seen them all, so you'd be ok with it." He smiles proudly, leaning against the edge of the door.

"Alright, Polo, where does this go?"

"Find out," he says, extending his hand toward the stairs. Before I step foot on the first stair, I turn on the light illuminating the burgundy runner and wooden steps. It is not much bigger than a closet, but not so tight where you would get claustrophobic. When I reach the top I see a wooden door with two deadbolts.

I undo the locks and push the door open, leading me onto a small wooden deck with a roof, lending to the most beautiful view of the city I could have ever dreamed of having. On the deck there are two wicker rockers with cushions and on the matching table, sits a bucket with ice and champagne. I walk up and pick up one of the glasses to see that they are engraved with 'Angel' and 'Polo'.

I giggle as I put the glasses back down and walk to stand at the rail as Logan walks up behind me, wrapping me in his arms.

"This is perfect," I whisper and take a deep breath, letting out a soft sigh. "Absolutely perfect."

ABOUT THE AUTHOR

B.C. Morin lives in Jacksonville Florida with her husband and two kids. When she isn't writing and spending time with her family she is learning to sew and making crafts. She released her debut novel Mark of the Princess in twenty-eleven and completed The Kingdom Chronicles series by releasing book three, *By The Sword* this year.

She is currently preparing to release her first New Adult novel entitled, *The Abiding*. A steampunk Victorian-era story that follows the life of Emeline Huntley and five others that are taken to fulfil a prophecy. They are turned into the ultimate killing machines using the better qualities of Vampires, Werewolves, and Nephilim. Emeline and the others are forced into the service of an aristocratic mad-man by means of clockwork collars with hidden blades sharp enough to cut through bone. But even clockwork collars cannot hold them for long......